Voices of Barnard Castle

Vol One

Voices of Barnard Castle
Vol One

Typesetting and cover design by Michelle Emerson
michelleemerson.co.uk

Voices of Barnard Castle

Vol One

A collection of poems, stories and memoirs
by members of the Barnard Castle Writers Group

Edited by
Raphael Wilkins and Emma Rowell

Barnard Castle Writers Group provides a forum which offers its members opportunities to receive supportive critical feedback on their writing and to give the same to other members.

In that and other ways, the group supports its members in achieving their individual writing aims across a wide range of genres.

More generally, Barnard Castle Writers Group aims to support initiatives which promote Barnard Castle as a literary town. The group welcomes new members. Its members share the leadership of its activities.

Contents

EMMA ROWELL

MAY TIME

I've got rowan, elder and hawthorn in my garden.
In May the blossoms, like wedding gowns,
Hang across their branches,
A delicate and intricate lacework.

I can smell the fragrance throughout the house,
The soap-powder freshness means
 Every day is wash day.

Tiny white flowers,
Make brides
Out of the trees and shrubs.
Attracting honey bees and bumblebees.
Who dance like bridegrooms,
To the tune the breeze brings.

Come autumn,
When the brides have lost their blooms,
And are lush, swollen and expectant,
The scene changes from innocence.
To this carnal place.
Dripping with blood-red berries,
Ripe in their shameless fecundity.

Then I'll pick the glossy rowan and elderberries,
Before the garden birds steal them all.
In a pan,
With fallen apples,
I'll boil and strain them.

Pouring the jelly into jars,
To eat at Christmas time.
When dark, cold nights
Make crones of the trees.

I'll light the fire
Put on the lamps,
In the chilly afternoon.
Taking out a jar of summer,
And remember foaming white branches.

The sleet will lash the windows,
As grimy twilight
Surrounds the house
And I'll open the jar and inhale
Busy bees and summer breezes.

On Christmas Eve,
The jelly is a baroque jewel
Red and gold,
Glowing in the lamplight,
Perfectly enhancing the aesthetic of the season.
But its sweet tang
Will return me,
To long, sultry evenings
In the garden,
Heady with the scent of flowers
And the hum of insects.

Then I'll long for summer.

Stargazing on Cotherstone Moor

Northern skies on a winter's night,
We are out on the moor,
Looking up.
Cold tears the breath from our lungs,
And the shock puts a rod through our backs.
We move like we are made of glass.
Brittle.

Starlight flickering, white,
Illuminating our view across the hilltop,
To witness the dark drama of night.

A fox screams its way into our consciousness.
The flock ahead move silently,
Towards the trees.
Occasionally we see the neon flash of their eyes.
Starlight moving through them.

Tonight we are part of this tenebrous theatre.
We are witness to the mystery of the night.
And wonder,
How?
Who made this?

When Demiurge ordered the chaos,
To forge all our physical world,
He looked to create Heaven.
He was a true craftsman, an artisan.

Forcing the rocks of the earth
To peak and trough,
Spinning threads of matter to furnish it gloriously,
In imitation of eternal forms.
Earth, Wind, Fire and Water.
Arranged tonight in perfect sameness,
So that we stand in that cold light,
Knowing that in those beams,
His work was made,
So distant and ancient,
Their beginnings.

Our circular journey is framed,
As the heavenly bodies continue across the night sky.
Some disappearing,
Behind the horizon, now.
We will see them rise again tomorrow.
Perfectly uniform
All the same,
Yet exquisitely different.
The rules that govern the chaos.

Our words leave us in a warm mist,
Instead of dissipating into the elements,
Of Wind and Water,
They become solid,
Settling around our scarves and collars,
Weight and substance.
Glistening like glass,
In the starlight.

SAN GIOVANNI'S EVE

I'm pouring honey onto roast walnuts,
On 24th June.

I've shelled them and their tight woody helmets are crushed,
Sharp on the board and floor,
Even the dogs stay away.

I tease the creamy morsel,
Out of its snug home,
By cracking the shell.
A tiny replica of the cerebral cortex,
In my hand.

It is said the nut in ancient times,
Was dedicated to Juno,
Who blessed a bride with fertility.

Walnuts were once thrown,
At the happy couple,
On their wedding day.
A cruel confetti since
With a fair aim,
The poor girl might,
Enter the conjugal state,
Bruised and tender.
A good preparation,
One might say,

"A woman, a dog,

And a walnut tree,
The harder you beat them,
The better they'll be."

As the old saying goes.

In Florence, in the middle ages,
Barefoot virgins,
Were made to climb up the walnut trees,
On the Eve of San Giovanni's feast day,
The Patron Saint of the city.
St John the Baptist, to us.

Whose head was separated,
From his body,
And put on to a platter,
Like my walnuts.

Glistening and delicious,
I take my walnuts,
Roasted, salted and glowing,
In amber honey,
To the table.
I set them down carefully,
Lick the sticky honey off my fingers,
And sit down.

I won't eat one,
In case I drop it.

Everyone knows that a witch cannot move,
With a walnut in her lap.

KITCHEN WINDOW

An upside-down pine cone,
Is tied to the apple tree,
Outside the kitchen window.
Between its woody scales,
Is a thick paste of nuts, seeds and lard.

It's an offering to our garden birds,
On this freezing cold morning,
The roof's frost mantle glitters hard.
No rich man's treasure is enough to capture this lustre,
It will be gone soon,
Once the sun,
Has made its way around the house.
Its glory washed into miry puddles,

Where the birds will gather,
To drink and chatter and reminisce,
About good times,
When they ruled this place.
When their grandfathers and grandmothers,
Ripped and tore through warm forests,
Bathed in shallow seas,
And celebrated their predominance,
With the blood, muscle and bones of lesser species.

Sparrows, blackbirds, wrens,
Dunnocks and starlings,
Gather there,
Nostalgic for the good times.

They joust and duel for raisins,
And breadcrumbs,
Dusted off the kitchen table.

Rich men take note,
These creatures now squabbling
and scratching for scraps,
Once ruled this world.
Their will shaped the green earth.
But nothing lasts and everything falls.
Great Ozymandias in Shelley's poem proclaims,
"Look upon my works, ye Mighty,
And despair"
Now his broken face and empty eyes,
Stare unblinking,
Across the dusty waste,
That has supplanted his past majesty.

Nothing lasts,
Everything falls,
Ye Mighty, Despair,

What will become of us?
When rich men,
Start to squabble and scratch,
For scraps?

Womb Dreams

I watched him sleep.
His womb dreams flicker across his eyelids,
The dark, watery shades,
Colour his expression.

With clenched fist and wide wet mouth,
He stirs,
Soft ozone breath rises,
As his voice takes its place in the air,
His new element.

All he will ever say,
His thoughts and deeds,
Are wrapped tightly within him,
He will become himself.

Sealed lids suddenly split,
To reveal a deep blue,
Ocean hue.
Inside his ancient soul,
All knowing, remembering.

He looks at me,
Calm and direct,
A long breath in,
As if, in preparation to speak,
But his eyes close again.

And he returns to his old place,

His sea life,
Curled tight like a cowrie shell.

TINNITUS

Sunlight dazzles me,
Through the window.
The patterns dancing on the floor boards,
Fool me into believing that,
Before me are islands and seas.

And me like Odysseus,
Hated by Gods and Men.

My voyage though short,
Is as troubled.

The shell against my ear spews out such terror.
Zeus has made me keeper of the winds,
My oxhide bag lays empty,
In the sitting room.
More than the west wind propels me now.
My presence brings destruction.
The flickering islands at my feet are wretched,
No one will be saved.

Poseidon screams and rises,
From the tumult at my feet,
He will not surrender his dominion,
Of these tempestuous waters.

So I turn back,
Defeated,
Returning to my favoured haunt and home,

In the sitting room,
Where curtains shade the sun,

My sanctuary,
"Yon close bound prison house of storms."

QUIET

I sat in the quiet of that room and remembered everything you had
  been.
The small, pale woman,
Underneath the hospital sheet,
Like a gentle church corner saint,
Is an interloper.

I close my eyes.

The cold hard sound of your silver bangles signals your arrival,
My heart is like a ball being kicked,
Against the wall of my chest.

Your voice,
Jagged in the air,
Cuts through,
Leaving a wound that bleeds,
Your mother's blood,
Vague and unanswerable.

On dark days,
Your eye refuses to reflect the lights.
In you a fire rages,
And we have to stand back to avoid the embers.
I'm happy to breathe in and out,
Near you,
Unseen.

I could never find the edge of you,

My eyes seemed incapable of seeing past you,
Your presence both comfort and terror,
Like a furnace burned us,
Furious and fierce,
Huge in my memory.

Now laid out,
Silent and wrapped in linen,
You seem peaceful,
Unrecognisable.
Your force has escaped you,
And is now stirring the sultry July afternoon,
Unseasonably bending the trees,
Whipping up the dust,
Into streaming eyes.

They will know you've gone.

Setting the Table one Christmas

All my cutlery is bought from junk shops,
EPNS and bone handled,

It is dropped at the shop,
Once the owners have passed,
And their death ceremonies are complete.

Then I own their bones,
I wash them,
And care for them,
I polish them,
And set them out on my table
To keep saint's days,
I surround them with food,
Flowers and candles.

In doing so,
Do I worship them?
With the initials of the dead,
Engraved onto forks and spoons,
Have the Smiths, Thomases and Browns,
become our household tutelary deities?

Should we expect them to protect us
From hunger?
Or hope that the souls of our dead,
Are taking time,
Whilst resting in perpetual light,
To look down upon us,

Here at this table/altar
And grant us our prayers?

Can they intercede for our sick,
Or make miracles happen?
Are we making the Marys, Mabels,
Peters and Johns divine?
Are they our holy intermediaries?

Should we revere them and ask,
Now they are in God's grace,
To ensure we have a long life
And come to join them in heaven,
Once we are dead like them?

No, this is idolatry.
And I'm going straight to Hell!

BROKEN BELLS

Smooth sheets soothe my skin
As I stretch out tired limbs.
No thoughts now,
Only the old themes,
Of food, sex and sleep,
Fill the space in my mind.
Gluttony, lechery and sloth,
So human,
Ungodly.

Darkness holds me
Incubi and Succubi
Are welcome,
If it means I'll sleep,
I'm too old to birth a witch.

I'll prepare for their night's visit,
With an 'Ave Maria'.

The church bells outside my window,
Sound three bells
Angelus?
Angelus Domini nuntiavit Mariae

My tongue like pieces of the true cross,
Sold without shame from the dusty Narthex,
Is solid and false in my mouth.
I cannot enter the peace within,
Until I've served my penance.

But my repentance goes unheard.

Life's sins too numerous to be washed away,
By these holy words,
Life is gluttony, lechery and sloth.

Now my bed linen's in knots,
My pillow like the veil of St Veronica,
I'll see all the stations of the cross tonight,
Praying for the sun to rise
And cleansing light to pour through the blinds,
Releasing me from this purgatory.

O Rex Gloriae Veni Cum Pace

MONSTERS

The clock on the mantelpiece,
Ticks his lazy song.
There's a fly at the window and her regular,
Slow beat, supplies some percussion.
It should be relaxing,
I should stretch out my legs,
Allow the pale, buttered sun to warm my limbs and slip me into
    sleep.

But there's bread baking
And soon the fragrance will fill the house,
Drawing the sleeping into the drama of the day.

Then there will be shouting,
Laughing, singing and teasing,
Tears, searches and
"Hurry ups",
With coats and kits and recorders,
We will sail out,
Scatter to the four winds
Across the moor,
The curlew cries his plaintive warning,

"Beware for here there be monsters".

ZERO
A L0VE POEM

Zero.
First recorded in the English Language in 1598,
A contraction of the Venetian, Zeverro,
Meaning *empty*.

In the West it is represented by 0
In the East by .
Zeverro,
Zefiro,
Zephyrus,
Sfir,
Zero,
0

.

I loved the very bones of you,
But you are gone,
And now I see the *empty* in both
L0ve as well as L0st

ALLY HAMMOCK

FOR THE LOVE OF LITTLE TERNS

Perhaps we are but Little Terns,
small and mighty hearted with
more resilience in our bones than
those that ride the wind above us.

Migrating through our separate lives
yet we charter the same brave course
and dream the same wild dreams
as we sleep on our wings.

Some days the white horses will
rise and rage and dance like
the claxons are sounding.
Some days the salty sea frets
will render us lost but,
I will always come back into view,
and you will too.

Then, maybe, if the tides align and
the moon dapples slight silver favour
at our feet then we will meet
on the forgiving shoreline

and see out the rest of the summers together,
two arrowed paper planes set free
where the shell-shingled earth
meets the grey North Sea.

SHE STANDS

Like the Rowan tree that cloaks itself
come October in her favourite autumn colours.
Close enough to lean upon slant silver
but distant enough that our independence
grows and flourishes like the wildflowers
and birds she teaches us about.

Rooting us in woodsmoke. Sustaining us with
homemade bread generously dolloped with
raspberry jam and love, as the storms roll in.
Wrapping arms, salted with sunspots
around our bodies when they feel broken
or our fractured hearts need fixing.

Cross stitching us back together by threading
words of comfort through our sea-fretting fears
and foggy tears, fledgling us on hope
even when dreaming skywards is hard
and wings are weighted with all that has passed.

We three fly onwards because she stands.

SKY-LINING

oh to be sky-lined
by you

tongue twisted inside out
by you,

tangled up in bones and
cornflower blue

unframed

untamed and

kissed right through.

THE SECRET BEACH

You were new once
a tiny slip of life in between
the creases of my dress.
All toes and fingers,
fuzzy nubbed like the willow.
Dimples like rock pools and
nesty blonde hair.
Born as the cornflowers and clover
scatter kissed the meadow and
the sun dawdled for days.

This is the place we'd sit when
my bones ached for sleep but
I was too in love to close
my eyes. You slant across
my heart beneath
the alabaster clouds and
ink blue sky.
Nestled in a forest of giant
celery leaves and
cow parsley skyscrapers
there was only you and me,

your mobile a kaleidoscope of
kingfishers and dippers,
damsel flies for stars and
the river your lullaby.

You Keep Me in Flowers

For most of life I feel as though
I am holding my breath tight,
in my chest. Cocooned in scarred
lungs, northeastern bones
and the summered olive skin
I inherited from Grandpa Len.

Then you walk into my room and
I exhale. Each breath emerges,
a kaleidoscope of colour.
Like the meadow come June, I am
buttercup yellow and cornflower blue
when you are in view.

SWIMMING IN THE TEES WITH MY DAUGHTER

We look at each other,
her eyes the colour of
the moor in autumn
and wild with youth—
mine compost green
so my dad always said,
and heavy with love
for this hipless bright like
kingcups in June,
Northeastern bairn, before me.

She smiles.
Her huge grin wide like
the sunrise, gappy toothed
and as beautiful as the skylarks
that sing, just out of view.
We pinch our noses with
trepidatious fingers and dive
into the copper rose
rust dappled waters
of the Tees.

The cold rises moonward
through our veins and
for a moment,
there is only us and
a thousand minnows.
A brief and watery
window of time in which
we get to be nothing
except alive together,

mother and daughter.

We burst again into the blue
like shooting stars,
exhaling the breath
clutched tightly in our lungs.
Bodies peppered with goosebumps
jelly legged we laugh like nothing
will ever worry us again
and relish this memory
we will always share,
to keep us warm when
the cold returns.

MARGARET ASQUITH

The Travel Bug

Nancy borrowed her brother's maroon polo neck jersey. It had a wee hole in the elbow, but that didn't matter because it had a cool shiny zip at the neck and would look trendy with her purple corduroy bellbottoms.

He'll be too busy to notice, consumed with his God and his new uni friends, she thought. It would do, and anyway, she didn't have much else. What do you take on a school skiing trip to Aviemore? she mused.

Now that Amy was working, she had nice things, all locked away in her wardrobe. The ugly sister, though she was pretty enough. You don't get to pick a sister, not like a best friend who knows you better than you know yourself. That's a fact, she thought.

She shut the bedroom door, a signal to Amy to keep out, and opened the old brown suitcase with a pang of excitement. Maybe she sensed that it would be the first of a lifetime of packing and unpacking her baggage.

Her eyes darted around the room with its twin beds, matching easy chairs, two of everything with an invisible line down the middle like a trench and never the twain shall meet. She wouldn't dare disobey and cross the enemy line.

She twirled in front of her side of the dressing table mirror, admiring her new maroon and purple outfit, fascinated to notice how her teenage frame was budding in all the right places. She added a long string of purple beads and big metal clip-on earring hoops from Woolworths. Cool.

They lived in a bungalow set in its own grounds with a lofty view of the rows of sooty council housing down the hill. Her dad's pride and joy. Her friends looked with envy at the smart house and their seeming idyllic lifestyle, belying the reality. It was her first time away without family, without the stotious Mum and Dad. They were mildly drunk most evenings, more on Fridays and she hated them for it with adolescent fury. She nursed that wrath and kept it warm all her life.

Finishing the packing, she remembered they'd been told they must take wellies, so she shoved them in the case last, pulled on her anorak and wandered out to the front drive where her best friend Anna and her mum and dad were waiting in their little Hillman Imp to take them to Waverley train station.

The house was quiet that morning like everyone was busy doing something else. Nobody in the family made a fuss or said much as she left. The family didn't do hugs then. Years later, the siblings learned how, though always awkwardly.

The case safely stowed in the boot, she climbed into the back seat with Anna. Anna's mum, always a sharp tongue, twisted round from the front seat and looked her up and down through a cloud of fag smoke.

"Did your mother not help you to get ready?" she rolled her eyes knowingly at the dad.

Nancy said nothing, noticing Anna's new anorak, smart jeans, pretty flowery wellies *on her feet*! She gulped back tears of embarrassment, thinking about her old green boots in the case.

As they drove down the high street, she wiped away the condensation on the window, watching people hurrying about their business in the relentless rain like wet ants. The town looked dismal as ever like it was mourning its coal mining heart. She saw the bright lights of the new supermarket where the excitement of shopping with a trolley and buying foreign foods like pizza and yoghurt was still the talk of the town months after the big opening. Across the road, Mr Banks in his greengrocer shop polishing his apples and lining up the colourful veg, looked beseeching at the shoppers like a forgotten grand old uncle.

Nancy sighed and sat up straighter, flicking back her long hair, thinking about the adventure ahead.

She caught the dad's eye in the driver mirror.

He winked.

The first in a lifetime of those kinds of winks. She would come to know them well. Her heart fluttered like a little giggle.

In the back seat, Anna linked their arms tightly, heads together, whispering their secrets like two pink sparklers waiting to be lit.

PEGGING OUT

I get a lovely sense of satisfaction when I see my washing flapping in the breeze. I love the freshly dried scent as it's brought in.

I first heard the Yorkshire term 'pegging out' when we lived in my husband's native Bradford. I had thought it meant someone or something (like your car) had gotten very old and died. "Ee lass", my kindly neighbour would say, "tha's not pegging out t'day? Luks lak rain ter me".

Fifty years ago, as a wee girl, I remember my mum Violet hanging out the family wash, as ever in her pinny, calf-length boots and housework turban (with three curlers peeping out on her brow). The display of bed sheets held up high on the washing line with wooden props looked like huge bunting snapping and cracking themselves dry in the howling wind of the Lammermoor Hills in our southeast corner of Scotland.

That same wind hurled us bairns down the road to school, my sister and I looking like rosy-cheeked banshees with our long hair blasted by the wind into horrid ringlets.

Mondays were always Mum's wash day, no matter the weather. If it was wet outside, she'd hoist the laden pulley in the kitchen to the ceiling and let the heat from the Aga get things dry, the room soon like a Glasgow steamy. She had set days when housework chores were done and that was that. It never seemed to occur to her or anyone to adjust to suit the weather. Same with our midday dinners, roast on Sunday, shepherd's pie Monday, fish on days when the fishman came in his van, with little variation. We walked home from school for dinner every day – usually three courses, all homemade of course. I never ever had a school dinner, and sometimes wonder if we missed out on the social side of that. I was never part of any wee gang and have watched from the side lines of the playground all my life.

Here in France, I often reflect on how pegging out is one of life's simple pleasures, like setting and lighting a log fire on a winter's day. That 'whoosh' sound as the kindling takes light. Perfect. All seems right with the world no matter where you are when you can peg out and light a fire. I love the ritual in the colder months of clearing out the ash from the day before, polishing the hearth, setting the fire ready for later, then around teatime, 'whoosh'.

We have taken the plunge and moved across the channel and our first French garden is mostly lawn with washing lines garlanded through the trees behind the house.

In the pretty village of Villemorin, I have an idyllic view of our neighbour's allotment packed with vegetables and flowers growing effortlessly weed-free. Monsieur Brassard, at 85, works his land not out of necessity (he is long retired and very wealthy) but because it's the French way of life, and that's what I adore, the love of the land, the care and attention to detail and the *fierté de leurs produits*. Monsieur B doesn't say much, just a nod and a smile, and there are little gifts of fresh vegetables, fruit or flowers left under our billowing sheets. Sometimes I hug myself with glee from the sheer pleasure of these simple things.

After six months we find ourselves dithering, in English of course, as we have only the bare basics of French, about whether we really like living in France or not. *Of course* we do, but while the house is open plan, beautiful and airy with exposed stone walls, it is freezing in the winter! We decide to stay in France and find another much cosier house, so we up sticks again and move to Deux-Sevres.

At the new house with its panoramic views, gazing down the valley to the Forêt de Secondigny is a glorious treat. Not only that, but I also have the company of three splendid free-range chickens who seem to find my pegging-out antics of great interest (or maybe it is amusement).

My working life started at the tender age of 15, with many lunch times spent in Edinburgh's Waverley train station absorbing the spirit of fellow travellers, longing to be one of them. At 18, I left home (my second attempt, but that's another story) 'to see the world' travelling alone to Montreal in Canada, lived there for a couple of years and have been roving it seems ever since. In over 40 years together, we have relocated many, many times around Scotland, England, Éire and France. We've bought, sold and sometimes renovated modern and old bungalows, farmhouses, terraces - we have done it all, mostly relocating through work opportunities.

Nowadays as a lifestyle choice, we choose to invest in adventure and travel rather than join the 'BaBaRi's (*buy-a-barn-and-renovate-it)* gang. Alright, there is an element of uncertainty and risk in renting, but it means enjoying our freedom and satisfying our gypsy wanderlust. We don't knock 'a home in the sun' ownership, but right now, it's not for us. We have found that we no longer share the British obsession with home ownership; thus we can take advantage of the huge and excellent value rental market here in France.

We both share the same exquisite thrill of moving into a new home, often someone else's, somewhere else, and now in another country, where everything is different, not just the language. The wind, the sun, the sounds, the light, the food and where the ordinary to-do list takes on a fun and challenging perspective. Even tackling the grocery shopping or the discovery that we cannot just transfer to another branch of the same bank, "*mais non madam!*" can be a baffling although enjoyable distraction. We love the differences, and maintaining our homely routines like pegging out helps banish any wee pangs of homesickness.

After more than forty years' of non-stop work, at last leaving my public servitude behind, I delight in having time for those tasks with a deep sense of peace and tranquillity. Not only that but on a practical level, pegging out costs nothing, reduces our carbon footprint by saving on energy bills, is aesthetically pleasing and smells divine!

I read somewhere that we can save around €20 a month by leaving the tumble drier switched off. It makes me wonder what the effect would be if everyone stopped using tumble driers. The sight of our washing merrily dancing on the line, to me, reflects humankind working hand in hand with nature and keeps me steady at the helm while we house-hop. There is something in my heart that yearns to peg out (the washing, that is) no matter where I am.

In the new place, we love to muse over some feature – the views, the strange furniture, bizarre wallpaper (on the doors and ceiling!), the garden, the essence of other people lurking in the corners and imagining the drama of their lives before us. The simple pleasure of poking about the new home never fails, and when the newness wears off or somewhere else beckons, we can pack the pegs and go.

Having de-cluttered several times, we have got it down to a fine art. As soon as we start toying with the idea of moving again, our things seem to line up and as if by magic, piles appear, lists start, boxes fill up and we find ourselves ready for *le déménagement*. Thankfully, tolerant family and friends think us nomadic pensioners a bit funky (or maybe a little bonkers). Our Christmas card list gets longer though, as we collect more friends who come to know us well enough not to be surprised when we announce another new address.

These winter months, we are house-sitting a holiday gîte just south of Toulouse while the owners take an extended trip to the UK. I adore the view of the pretty snow-capped Pyrenees in the distance and picturesque hilltop villages galore as I peg out. We like it so much we have already found and secured our next new home in the Tarn and move there in the spring. From there, we plan to explore the midi Pyrenees for a year or two as well as house-sitting around Europe. I am looking forward to wash days there!

Maybe our alternative lifestyle is not for everyone. The buzz of retiring a bit early, selling up lock, stock and getting rid of the barrels (that is the hardest bit), moving with our dwindling chattels to strange new places, leaving the familiar, the 'what if' and 'what's next'; it's hard to beat. Now, where did I put those pegs?

WHAT'S NOT TO LOVE?

The main road into Barnard Castle is one of the best town gateways I have seen. When you leave behind the busy A66 with constant traffic zooming east and west as the Romans did (maybe not so fast), you are immediately transported into idyllic rural prettiness on a country road wending its way past 17th century Rokeby Park, over the 250-year-old Abbey Bridge and then treated to a stunning view of the ruins of 12th-century Egglestone Abbey. What a welcome!

The first time I travelled this way to Barney, I was immediately smitten with the place and that was before I saw the bustling market on the Horsemarket cobbled street, the well-preserved castle ruins and the skyline of chimney pots jostling their way past the Butter Market Cross down the bank to the River Tees like gossiping old grandees. The place is oozing historical intrigue, charm and delight.

My amused neighbour, Mrs P, looked at me quizzically after hearing about my ex-pat jobs and house hopping over the last forty or so years living at over thirty different addresses. "Are you a fugitive?" she asked.

Well, no. I'm not running away but perhaps towards something more that will probably never be found, but whatever that is, Barney ticks an awful lot of boxes. Thankfully, nowadays, those links are easily maintained through various social media, unlike back in the 1970s, when working as an au pair in suburban Montreal, I'd stand at the window every morning watching for the *Postes Canada* bringing those treasured blue airmail letters from home.

My dreams of travelling in fabled faraway lands were just starting to unfold. The island of Montreal, to me, a wee Scottish lass, was and still is, the epitome of modern sophistication with its glittering skyscraper skyline, Quebecois culture, and dazzling state-of-the-art underground shopping centres joining up the subway system. It was full of mystique to me, and I adored the role of passer-by, an outsider looking in, always have and always will. I've never tried to get inside the world of other people, but rather be the on-looker 'who sees most of the game', as my dad used to say. Observe and leave the commenting to others, bow to the 'high heid yins' was his good advice. Now, so many places, adventures, near catastrophes, and some mischief later, where better to linger and reflect than the glorious northeast, surely the real centre of Britain in many respects. I'm drawn here after years of longing for something without really knowing what it was.

I'd delight in the bustle of travellers dashing across the marble foyer, some disappearing through the revolving doors leading into the magnificent North British Hotel and the echo of announcements for far-bound trains. Oh, how I longed to be such a traveller.

Whatever you look for and find in life, happiness, I think however you define that, is being at peace with yourself, being content, having hope and good people around you and practising the universal religion of kindness and giving that heals past wounds, however made. The people of Barney and nearby villages are mainly farming stalwarts born from centuries of traditions and beliefs. You can see this at any of the summer agricultural shows when several generations of the same families gather to celebrate; although slightly bowing to the might of change, as we all must, they are carefully preserving ancient spirit and courage.

Barney has a nice, friendly feel to it, where every day, the many cafes are filled with people chatting to each other easily. The town is like a grand old lady sitting discreetly behind the scenes in the land of the Prince Bishops. Lots of visitors are drawn by the history, the wonderful French-styled Bowes Museum, great eateries, walking trails galore, theatre, the annual Meet, local flora and fauna, architecture and general holiday atmosphere. I always feel like I'm on holiday when I'm in town like I'm just passing through. Anyway, this is a good place just to be, even for fugitives!

Out With the Old

Albert Reece sighed deep in thought, deaf to the faint hum of the fridge, the ticking of the clock, and two jiggling eggs in the pan, although he did notice the delightful bird song from the garden. It was a beautiful spring day at number 22, but even that didn't lift his spirits.

Today, he was taking Gladys to the Care Home for a trial two-week stay. She seemed not to mind and had talked every day this week about looking forward to her 'holiday'. He dreaded how she might react when he left her there.

One armchair.

One single bed.

One set of cutlery.

One teapot – one cup.

How long till she realised? Would she ever? She already treated him as a stranger. So distant. Maddeningly polite at times.

Where was the old feisty Gladys? She has commanded respect for decades as the Head of Oxby Grammar, and now look at her, fussing over her clothes as she packed, folded, and re-folded.

If the truth be known, he felt shameful relief. The burden of looking after her had become too much. There was no fun anymore. No more trips to the theatre. He couldn't bear having to explain what was happening, she seemed always distant in another world. He repeated everything – so tiresome, she showed no interest.

Now who would look after him? Well, there was Doris two doors down, she did a tasty steak and kidney, and Mary across the road loved to share a jigsaw. He was only 75, plenty life left in him yet and they saw him as a safe bet. Yes, as Sergeant Reece, he'd pounded the beat around here for as long as most could remember and even now, they still called him Sarge.

The estate, once a proud post-war council showpiece of some 600 semis, was slowly declining into a shabbier rebel state. Graffiti unseen a decade ago now peppered the landscape, and local shopkeepers were forced to shutter their premises in ugly metal. But the old-timers like Albert still kept their regulation privets determinedly trim. The bandits hadn't won yet and the pebble dash had survived the brutal coastal weather. Mind you, being on the seafront was still a sure sign of success, not like some of the backstreets where he had dealt with many a domestic. Not just the locals but these Scottish holidaymakers too. Once they got drinking, all hell would break loose. He chuckled to himself, thinking of the unholy skirmishes he'd had to sort out. All it took was a word of warning in those days.

He heard Gladys coming down the stairs.

He gasped as she appeared in the doorway – she looked amazing! He'd not seen her in that pretty dress for years and her best handbag, the one she kept for good. Crikey, she must have forgotten where she was going. As usual he said nothing. He took her case out to the car, being careful not to step on her treasured seashells lining the path. The gulls overhead squawked louder than ever. By God, these birds got bigger every year. Must be all those scavenged fish and chips, he thought wryly.

Gladys followed him out and settled quietly in the passenger seat, looking a bit flushed, her eyes bright like a kid going on a trip. Where on earth did she get that garish crimson lipstick? He'd never seen her wear that before. She really was losing it, he sighed.

She didn't even look at the house as they left – 46 years in that semi, she might never see it again! Oh well. He waved to Mary, who just happened to be out on her driveway as they passed. By heck, she *was* a fine-looking woman and looking pretty today, and there was Doris bending over to pick out some weeds with a rather fetching little wiggle. He glanced at Gladys, but she had that faraway look again.

They arrived at 'Devine Homes' just after lunch and soon had Gladys safely settled in her room. Actually, quite a nice setup, thought Albert, very comfortable indeed, and the sea views are amazing.

"Well bye-bye, dear," said Gladys. "I'll see you soon."

She didn't seem to care that he was going and leaving her there. He suddenly felt a bit glum, awkward.

She was refreshing her lipstick!

"Right, I've got to go," she said. "There's a tea dance this afternoon and Jim will be waiting for me. Remember Jim from number 44? Well, he is here too. I'm so glad he let me know this room was available. Bye, dear."

Albert's jaw dropped and so did the penny.

GONE TO SEED

The brown paint-chipped door of the shed hangs slightly loose on its hinges, catching the breeze and banging gently. The cobweb-shrouded window embraced by weary end-of-season honeysuckle allows just enough light to glimpse the neatly stacked terracotta pots, labels, ties, string, dibber, and bulb store waiting on the back wall. The hint of a warm, comfortable place to sit on rainy days and dream and sigh contentedly.

Three inviting wooden steps, worn smooth by decades of heavy tread, lead to the path made from bricks squirrelled away over the years from a derelict mill that gives a splendid blaze of earthy hue punctuating flowering fountains of scent and colour.

Scarlet poppies, white marguerites, lavender, blues, pinks, tall and small, and wild, wild flowers bursting to show off, all fighting to bow respectfully and kiss the path where the slow, heavy steps once plodded by, trailing fag smoke, creak, creak from the old wooden wheelbarrow.

At a crossroads of paths, framed in stunning red and green mass, beans on canes against a blue sky triumphantly herald the beauty yet to come. A myriad of vegetable cousins lined up as if for inspection, round fat turnips, pale shy cauliflowers, waxy dreamy potatoes, blushing beetroot, cute carrots, florets of broccoli, globes of tasty onions – a whole floor show like young dancing hopefuls waiting to be picked but never chosen.

Against the fence lies a child's ball, sun-bleached, rejected by impatient young visitors with their iPads, but left there as a reminder of happy times, perhaps in the hope of new ownership one day.

In the middle of a half-dug row of potatoes, the fork is still stuck forlornly in the ground, serving dutifully as a prop for the gardening jacket, recycled from its days in the city, pockets bulging with handy string, trowel, rags, lighter, smooth pebbles, old pennies. Treasures that were never thrown away.

The blackbirds eye the jacket suspiciously, sensing its permanence now, and the weeds creeping in stand solemnly to attention as if they know their turn to rule has come.

The Old Ones are the Best

Reg Brown felt he was getting too old for business meetings, but the lads had persuaded him to attend; he would be the 'honorary' guest, they said, with a good booze-up after. The fact is, they just don't need me anymore, and they are making sure I go. Retirement here I come! he thought wryly.

He was worried about June, though. He just had a gut feeling that she wasn't happy. Alright, she was 20 years younger than him, but he was sure that now, with more time together, they could keep their union stronger than ever.

He checked into the hotel. Wow, not bad! Wall-to-wall glass, plush carpets and sheer luxury furnishings. The lads had gone to town on this. These upmarket hotels were all about pampering. He selected a Laphroaig single malt from the mini bar, sank down into the jacuzzi, tuned into The Archers to catch up on the stalwarts of Ambridge and sighed deeply. Well, this is the life, he smirked to himself. Only one thing missing and that was June.

He reached for the in-room Bluetooth keyboard and wrote her a message, wishing he'd his reading glasses to hand. This wasn't his preferred way to communicate, but he felt she might appreciate his attempt to speak in her digital world. He wiped away the steam, picked her email address and clicked 'send'. She'd love all this, he thought contentedly.

Over on the other side of town, Jane Brown let herself into the house, listening to the silence. She felt a huge relief to be alone at last with her thoughts. The service had been beautifully done, but the gathering of so many mourners had been a painful endurance, especially all her friends and family trying their best to comfort her. Words were useless to her right now. She looked around the lounge. Everything was tidy, just as she'd left it. She would never have believed she would miss his mess. He was the type of man who walked into a room and it was instantly untidy. His larger-than-life personality, his high-octane approach to life that was almost childish in its craziness. She had found his ideas endearing and ridiculous, scary and delightful. She'd never thought about missing him, not really. Nothing prepares you for this. She stifled a sob and sank down into the couch.

Just then, her laptop pinged to herald yet another message. She frowned and sighed. She didn't want condolence cards, but social media messages were so far out of her sphere. It was a strange world these days. She clicked on the new message, screamed and passed out.

Outside the house, Jake parked in the double driveway in his father's spot. He'd felt uncomfortable leaving his mum on her own tonight of all nights. She had coped so well and despite all her protestations that she was alright, he just wanted to be sure. He frowned, seeing the curtains undrawn, no lights on. He was unsettled seeing the house like this. His dad had been steadfast in his habits, always checking blinds, curtains, doors, lights. He would have thought Mum would do the same after all these years.

He found his key and went in. Switching on the lounge lights, he was shocked to see Mum lying on the floor. She was breathing and coming round. She had the laptop in her arms. He looked at the screen.

'To my loving wife, I know you will be surprised to hear from me like this. They have computers here and we are allowed to send emails to loved ones. I have just checked in. How are you and the kids? This place is very nice, but I am lonely here. I have made the necessary arrangements for your arrival tomorrow. I am expecting you darling, can't wait to see you.'

A NEW YEAR RESOLUTION

The best thing about New Year's resolutions, thought Emily, was making a list. There was something satisfying about writing it down. It was as if you had already achieved that goal. It was a start. If there was one thing that had steadfastly kept her going through hard times (very hard times indeed) it was a list. She might suggest that to others as a good resolution. It would be your conscience, your best friend and confidant and the one to reproach you when some task wasn't done. It wasn't on the list!

Emily looked appraisingly in her mental mirror, delving deeper than usual. Well, there was a lot more of her if she was being honest (and she was). No point getting a bigger mirror or bigger clothes, So the first resolution on her list:

Eat sensible healthy food
and no more delicious home-made cake.

She wrote that down.

It was a good resolution, no doubt. She reflected on this time last year (and the year before that), yes there was an echo of the same resolve. What had gone wrong? she mused. Was wrong, the right word? She was still the same person. She was not a bad person. She had done nothing wrong, as such. She *was* a bit uncomfortable if the truth be known. The fact was she lacked willpower and she loved her sweet treats.

She decided to think of another resolution.

Stop finding fault in others. That was a good one. Much though she loved her family and friends, it was far too easy to be critical and see the errors in their ways when a kind word over a nice cup of tea and a bit of encouragement would make the real difference. She knew that but, maybe just maybe, she needed to practice this more. She thought of the odd occasions when she had allowed a harsh word (or two) to slip out and regretted it, covering her faux pas with some nicer remark when it was too late. You can't take the words back. We all have our faults, she sighed.

She put the kettle on and warmed the teapot, resisting the cake tin seeming to shine brighter than usual on the shelf. She loved nothing better than sharing a cuppa and a good natter over her well-worn kitchen table by the Aga.

Then, she had a flash of inspiration. That's it! Drink more tea and be kind. That was all the resolution she needed.

WHEEL OF FORTUNE

The old radiogram can often be heard playing 'Wheel of Fortune' by Kay Star, lamenting time and again as if she needed reminding that it had not spun for her.

The lopsided curtains, useless against the cold damp air from the open window, clash with the dry blast of heat from the electric fire.

Rank smoky air, unable to mask the stench, mingles with sickly lavender room freshener. Across the wide doorframe, scratches in the wood tell tales of awkward wheelchair passage. The carpet in front of the fireplace is pitted with ciggie burns where the chair settles as if in grooves to face the telly.

Spectacles smeared from grubby fingers perch on a head of long grey nicotine-stained hair that has outgrown the ghastly perm she never wanted. A set of pristine false teeth lie unworn on the dusty mantelpiece amongst treasured mementoes from happier times. The dentist had frowned examining the worn gums unfettered for years, knowing it was a wasted exercise. Worth it, though, she had thought with a gummy grin for the 'Dial-a-ride' taxi into town and being pushed in her clapped-out chair by her exasperated daughter-in-law.

On days when 'Wheel of Fortune' is unbearable, Channel Four Racing commentary bellows encouragingly from the telly. She squints through one eye to watch the horses, distracted for a while from her doleful thoughts, the other eye blinded by smoke belching from the Embassy Regal at the corner of her mouth, missing the spectacles perched forgotten on her head. The kindly warden, believing the tales of family neglect, dubiously places her bets, keeping her gambling secret.

She sighs deeply. Nothing to look forward to other than getting her cataracts done and the wry pleasure of watching the stern carer as she:

Shuts the window.

Turns down the fire.

Tut, tut.

Tidy, tidy, tut, tut.

Turns down the volume of the telly.

Tidy, tidy.

Some days, without warning, she is plunged into a bath with bubbles to hide her old body and left to soak and brood, feeling like a helpless fish in a tank. She smirks sourly to herself at the thought of growing fins from spending what seems to her far too much time in the water.

The evening winter light casts shadows over the old furniture, polished with pride in its day, salvaged years ago from the shameful divorce. Now it sits grotesque in this dismal, sheltered world where her limbs no longer support her, speech is laboured and pride is best denied.

Resentful tears like jewels catch on the wrinkles and twinkle in the lamplight as she dozes, dreaming of what might have been.

SOMETHIN'S BREWIN'

The flames flicker in the breeze
as embers glow and fade and intensify
like the entrails of secrets revealed in the grate.
They gazed at the fire joined in exile
the coals holding the truths that divide.
The old one, she who knew,
cast a cunning eye in the dying light that defied escape.
The wind got lower, distant owls screeched and then silent,
The old tin kettle humming
Fusions of hot leaves brimming,
each their faded cups drenched in past passions of time
and more to tell and more to hear.
Drawing out their words once never spoken,
At last, at last, the tea was made
let them begin.
The women swayed, faltered, grew stronger
whispered, nodding at the moon, bright with resolve.
The Grumpy Old Women's AGM was ready to begin.

SPRING

Fresh
green, bright
lemon, yellow, daffodils
gusty winds that thrill
snowdrops, crocus, hyacinth, galore, and
easter bunnies, chickens, songs, family, more
walks, hills, mucky boots, picnics, friends, *j'adore*
hints of summer, warm, lush, growth, seed potatoes
decorating, changing, cleaning, holidays, good gatherings, let's do
  it
energy, new light, lambs, rain, rain, it's England, you know

SOMEBODY

"**I** could have been somebody, you know," Val would often say.

Well, she was someone.

She married once and loved twice.

Her son was a small-bit TV actor, and when he married, Val was sworn to secrecy that the event was to be covered by *OK!* magazine.

She told me, asking, "Can you keep a secret?"

And before I could answer …

"Well, you know our Harry? He's getting married to Jessica on the xx Game Show. The wedding is going to be covered by *OK!* magazine. Now, mind you don't tell anyone. I love you, you know."

I nodded, acquiescent as ever to Val's requests.

Like the time she decided to go to the local pub on a Saturday night, dressed as a chicken. I never told a soul. The element of surprise (we were all supposed to guess who it was) perfectly enacted by the crowd. Everyone knew and loved her.

Sometimes, she'd appear in a feather boa wearing it like you or I would wear a scarf.

One time, she danced and danced in her leprechaun suit at a St Patrick's night party.

She was found the next day, sitting in her favourite chair with the well-thumbed *OK!* magazine on her lap.

Rest in peace, Val. I miss you.

You were somebody.

Start from Scratch

I took two young grandsons to visit a neighbour who has a garden of Eden-like qualities. Having toured the amazing vegetables and flowers, shrubs and trees, the boys were delighted as baby frogs jumped over their shoes and to see chickens wandering freely, pecking and scratching the ground, looking for tasty morsels.

The new chicks had only been let out of their hutch that day, a week after being rescued from cage rearing with its severe confines.

As they waddled about the garden in the sunshine, they looked both wretched and deliriously happy.

Their coats were bald in patches, some misshapen feathers sticking out, but you could see on their faces a look of utter happiness, or was it relief?

The biggest one waddled across and rubbed her beak against my leg. She must be blind, I thought, till she looked up and winked at me.

She seemed good-natured and the boys were charmed. I had warned the boys not to frighten the poor chicks and to be prepared for some hostility as they would have to learn to trust their rescuers, but we had nothing to worry about. The other three made their way to us lopsided, pecking, squawking and a bit squinty-eyed.

"I think they are behaving very well," said my kind neighbour.

Not surprising, I thought, free from suffering a vile life and made welcome in a safe place with endless prospects to start from scratch!

LINDA BIRD

LILY AND ALFIE MEET SANTA AT 'THE BOWES'

Been bored, bored, so bored,
But today is filled with excited chatter.
What will he really look like?
What will he say, and they will tell him…
So many wishes this year.

Lily pinches Alfie and he pinches her.
They really are at 'The Bowes'?
They race each other through the gates,
There are market stalls and people!
Children and parents laughing and smiling,
Mum shouts, "Keep your distance."

People are dancing without music,
Keeping apart and together at the same time
The choir's voices ring out clearly,
"Ding, Dong Merrily on High in Heaven the Bells…."
Eyes glowing with delight, they skip along.

It really is Christmas, where can Santa be?
When will it be their turn to meet him?
This is one promise Mum and Dad can keep,
So many have become hopes.
Hope that they can play out with their friends.
Hope that they can see Gran 'In Real Life'.

Visiting Santa is important, so important.
They race up the grand steps to the museum,
Alfie catches a glimpse of Santa -

"He is in his own tent, oh! and there are elves."
Lily squeezes Mum's hand, Alfie jumps up and down.
This promise has come true, they will see Santa.

Families are queuing in little groups,
The chief elf calls them to walk up to Santa's tent.
He is the perfect Santa, he is real, he is here.
Nothing else exists just Lily, Alfie, and Santa.
They chat happily with him for a few minutes,
He asks what they are hoping for this Christmas.

They look at each other, they look at him,
Both blurt out "to hug Grandma".
Then they remember about wanting new bikes,
But hugging Grandma is the most important!
Oh! but they must wait for it to come true.
So instead, they'll tell her she's the best gran, and they love her.

Teasdale Wins Through in 2020

2020 will not be forgotten
We want to consign the experience to history
How we are surviving is a bit of a mystery.

Young and old feel out in the cold,
Front-liners and volunteers have broken the mould
Giving broad shoulders for others to cry on,
And helping hands for us to rely on.

We lost the best of us, the rock of our family, the old and the frail.
Yet we kept our resolve and stayed strong for those around us,
Delivering medicines, food and good cheer up and down the dale,
Telephone chats to raise the spirits so no one is alone.

As Christmas draws near and we are in the third tier,
We are all keeping our distance from our nearest and dearest.
Our volunteer groups have swung into action,
Delivering hope to people on our farms, in villages and towns, giving
their best.

NHS, shopworkers, carers and frontline staff working through the
  season
Will give us the confidence to enjoy Christmas with family and
  friends
(In a 'socially distanced way', of course!)

My plea is that this time next year, we'll all be vaccinated and
  COVID-19-free.
From myself and all involved with TAP, we wish you all good cheer
And hope that for each of you, Santa is near!

ONE-NIGHT STAND

It wasn't a starry night
more wet, snowy and frosty;
hubris and loss colliding.
Sitting Buddha-like, smug and serene
cocooned in bedding, cardboard and plastic.
A one-night stand with self and conscience.
Fairy lights to read by, hot water bottle for warmth.
Sharp shrill voices cut through the night;
pub to bar, bar to pub, late-night hot food.
Before dawn, in the silence, for a moment
it felt like it could be every night.
The cold penetrating to the bone
despair and fear your bedfellows.
As the dawn breaks, you contemplate
another night, no food, no bed, no home.

SUNDAY IN THE RED LION

Some days we feel abandoned
The thread of life frayed
People barely connected
In the village alone

But on a Sunday afternoon
The threads are twisted together
In that small room
We show our love of life

It starts with twos or threes or fours
Talk of last night, last week
What was on the telly or the football
The best brews or the usual

The individual conversations
Slowly become entwined
Punctuated by low guffaws
High-pitched ripples of laughter

The moment is reached
It's a communal conversation
A joke about a shared acquaintance
Or a dig at the Government

This light-hearted reverie restores
It makes local and visitor alike
Part of our community
On Sunday we are revitalised

THE DOGS ARE CALLING

It is a midsummer night, and
the sky glows in the northwest.
The dogs call across the valley
back and forth, back and forth.
Work done this is their time,
the call of the wild in every sinew.
As darkness descends; owls twit twoo,
and still the dogs are calling.
A dog slips its collar.
He races down the field to the wood,
fords the river through the wood and
up the field to the farmstead.
She calls him to her, "I'm ready".
They greet, sniffing and scenting
until the moment of their tryst.
It overwhelms and consumes them.
When it is over their muzzles touch
He is off and must return home.
He remembers this is a dangerous time;
this is not his territory and farmers have guns.
Will he make it home tonight?
Or is it the night the farmer wakes?
As dawn approaches the dogs fall silent.

The Tenors

Sitting in the back row
Il Divo's voices aquiver
The years peel away
Something is said; they snigger

Now the tenors' voices soar
Was that the right note?
Or did someone ignore?
"Listen please listen" is the plea

A random note is heard
"What did you say? We misheard"
The sopranos trill their thing
"When do we come in?"

Peering over her glasses
She listens to hear their best notes
"Oh yes! It was so nearly"
And then there's a sweet sound

"You see" they say in unison
"You can't do without us.
The basses are two-a-penny,
We're worth a million"

The sopranos turn around
Look them up and down
Then in unison they cry
"Boys will be boys"

IN THE BYRE WITH DAD

Early morning sun hits grubby windows
Inside the cattle shuffle in their stalls
Familiar smells of sweet grassy breath
High notes of meadow hay and cow dung
Mingle in the warmth from their bodies
Soft pulsating sounds of the milking machines
Dad, his shirt sleeves rolled up, tends the cows
There he is at one with the animals
Listening to their sounds and movements
An old battered radio stands high on the windowsill
Its sounds mingle and blend in the air
'Puff the Magic Dragon', 'Catch a Falling Star', 'Que Sera Sera'
We children stood watching, listening, learning, feeling
Little knowing that these moments would live on
Through us when you are gone

VALERIE BUCKNALL

TEN THOUSAND THINGS

When I reflect the light that shines on me
I am a mirror, moon to some great sun.
I cast a shadow, I am like a tree
and in this forest, stand with everyone.
We stand and grow, and shelter little birds
while insects crawl and rabbits hop about
and all things speak. They are the very words
expressing... what? They whisper and they shout,
they sing, they murmur. They are here to say
"We are the world, created here and now.
Look well," they warn, "this is our little day,
but if you look, you may discern somehow
that this is a projection on a screen,
of something that, without us, is not seen."

FAME AND FORTUNE

With all my noble thoughts and verbal skill
I would not write a sonnet, no not I,
I'd write a novel, and perhaps I will.
In fact I think I'll start one by and by
As I have seven hours a week to kill
and a computer, I shall have a try.
I've read some how-to books, I know the drill
And once I've found a plot, I'm home and dry.
The Booker Prize is well within my reach
and being famous would be rather fun.
I'll make my fortune easily, I know.
They'll flock to hear me when I make a speech
and cheer and clap me when the speech is done
then you'll remember that I told you so.

CONTAINMENT

I thought that I was drowning in my tears
and washed away in floods of dreadful fears.
Imagination ran away with me
out of control, as now I plainly see.
I made a picture, set it in a frame.
If this occurred again, I'd do the same.

SNOWBOUND

I'm a fully accredited snowman
with a first-class honours degree
of twenty at least below freezing.
If you were to cuddle me
I would melt in your arms in a moment
soaking you through and through
and then I'd be nobody nowhere
and *you* wouldn't know what to do.
Don't cuddle a qualified snowman.
I'm sorry, I have to say "pass",
but in spring I might change to a snowdrop
and peep at you out of the grass;
then you might gently approach me
admiring my delicate form.
Until then... Shall I tell you my secret?
Can you guess? Are you getting quite warm?
'S no wonder I'm frigid and chilly
and dread the spring thaw and the rain.
I need to be numb. It's not silly.
It keeps me from feeling my pain.

Not Avoidant

The word 'attachment' makes my blood run cold
for we are all detached when we grow old
if not before. Now I was cut adrift
before my birth, and none can heal the rift.
Not waving, no, nor drowning, here I stand
upon an isle with trees and silver sand.
Your ship passed by, I wished you'd come ashore,
but then I wished you wouldn't even more.
Ambivalent attachment? Anxious? Yes.
I write these lonely words in my distress.

AN OBSERVER

I spoke to my brain.
I said, "You work very hard."
He was going like a machine,
wheels turning, pistons pumping;
steam was coming out of his ears;
there was an ominous hissing sound.
"My function is to keep
everything
under control"
he panted.
"I must keep
my mind
on the job
or there could be
a serious
malfunction.
I must check on everything.
If a small detail is
forgotten
a disaster could occur,
and I should be held
responsible."
"Pardon my saying this,"
I observed,
"but there is one small detail you have overlooked."
"Oh my goodness,
what's that?"
He looks exhausted and worried.
"If you don't rest
and let the whole thing cool down,
it will all blow up."

"You're right," he said.
"Will you keep an eye on things
while I have a break?"
"OK, don't worry," I said
"I'll be around."

IN THE KITCHEN

This is the day, this is the hour,
here is the salt, there is the flour,
this is the butter, those are the eggs,
this is the bottle, I am the dregs.
Where is the wine? Where is the jam?
Empty the jar, and empty I am.

TRUTH DRUG
OR VIA DOLOROSA

Illusion makes you ill.
Swallow this bitter pill.
Swallow your bitter fate.
It is too late
to put the matter right.
Shed bitter tears at night
and in the day
go on your bitter way.

ABSENCE

It fills my mind like cotton wool,
like a cloud blotting out the sun
It stares at me blankly,
gives me no space
to explore other possibilities.
It consumes my energy
pins me to the chair,
and I sink down
under its weight.
The day is long,
long.

ADRIFT

I don't know
what to do
I don't know
how to behave
if you don't talk to me.
If you talk I listen
I learn what you like.
If you are silent
I am at sea
adrift
in my uncertainty.

MESSAGE

It's hard
to send a card
when you're half-dead
on the sea-bed.
It reads, not
'Wish you were here,'
but
'Wish you could hear.'

Maybe Tomorrow

When the sun shines
I'll sew cushions
turn out rubbish
hoover and dust
Maybe even
write a novel!
But not today.
It's cloudy.

So Sorry

My head
is full of lead.
my feet
lose their grip;
my back
swings to the horizontal.
Whatever happens
I must take it lying down.
Can't you help me?
Can't you *do* something?

So sorry, no.
My hands are tied.

PARTING WORDS

Dear world, why don't you
come halfway to meet me?
I have tried
God knows
to fulfil your requirements
to meet all the needs
in the hope that at last
my own would be respected.
But no
the demands are insatiable
and I, unseen,
am drained of resources.
I must plead poverty
ill health, exhaustion.
I must live in retirement
and let you pass me by.

GRIEF

Nothing grew
in the lonely gardens of my heart.
My brainforest was cut down
By sharp words;
all the birds had flown.
In the sour and sluggish river
no fish swam.

My world almost died
for want of your smile.
If you had been happy
I'd have flourished.

DOT

When time runs backwards
as they say it may one day
the dot will have her way;
not wishing to be here
she wants to disappear;
instead of growing,
she'll be going
down in size
to her surprise.
She'll decrease
then rest in peace.

MOURNING AT MIDNIGHT

At midnight mass the people sing
Gloria
a child is born.
At the back Dolores sits weeping
- a child is born
to suffer.

'Weep for yourselves
and for your children;
weep for the Holy Innocents;
and by the way Dolores
since you live to tell the tale
do not use biblical language
but pictures of children
in Romania, Cleveland,
Soweto, Bromley,
and hold up a mirror,
reflect the child within.'

GULF CORMORANT

My God becomes
what I am,
what you are;
shares it,
experiences it,
unites us with each other
and to everything human,
everything animal,
vegetable, mineral…
God becomes
the air, the sea
and that bedraggled bird
with its message
'See me, love me, know me;
break down barriers,
enter into peace.'

FEAR

Fear is about anger.
Anger is about pain.
Pain is about love.
Love is about everywhere
but we don't always see it.

ANGELS FEAR TO TREAD

A thing is so, and also is not so.
The things we know, we also do not know,
and what we do not know, and don't suspect,
we ought to treat with care and great respect.

EASTER

Oh how I longed for the shining face of love
to rise like a sun over the horizon of my life,
to rise in power and beauty
lighting my heart,
my whole world, with happiness!
This was my dream
as I lay waiting, waiting.
The night was cold and long;
I lay looking and listening;
too cold, too long!
I despaired of the dawn,
almost died of the darkness.

Now, thankful for morning,
I am drenched in healing light,
bathed in well-being,
saved by your smile.

CREATIVITY

On life's stage
scene shifters are at work.
In the landscape of the mind
mountains rise
out of a sea of tears;
molten rock streams down,
the ground moves and shudders.

Houses fall.
Shall we build others?

The curtain falls.
Shall we write a new play?

A MOVING EXPERIENCE

Baby Kanga in the pouch;
when she jumps he mutters, "Ouch!"
Sharing every tummy rumble,
safe and warm, he doesn't grumble.

Monkey jumps from tree to tree;
baby says, "Look after me!"
tightly clings to Mummy's fur,
never to let go of her.

I feel seasick when you move,
happier in rut or groove.
I'll be good; will you be kind?
I'm frightened I'll be left behind.

Most Irregular

Can I afford to be this happy?
Only for a little while.
I'll snatch at it quickly
before I return to duty.
It's like parking on a yellow line.
I keep glancing back
to see if the warden's coming.

SECRET THOUGHT

This little girl is far too good;
she acts exactly as she should.
She wears a smile, she's neat and clean;
this is the way she should be seen.
But no one sees her heart, where she
is just a slave. She is not free.
Her secret thought she can't admit;
she's bound to be a hypocrite.
She grows in body and in mind.
Her secret thought is left behind.
Her smile is false, and cold as frost.
She does not know what she has lost.
Her secret thought was life and fire.
Without it she has no desire
for anything, except to please.
May God help women such as these!
They act exactly as they ought
and do not know their secret thought.

SURVIVAL

I try to please you
the way a flower
which turns to face
the light
is trying to please
the sun.

ISOLATION HOSPITAL, SCARLET FEVER 1947

A sick child in the bed.
Is it a cold in the head?
Is it a pain in the tum?
No. All she wants is her mum.

The fever won't leave her.
Her throat and her ears
are trying to tell them
but nobody hears.

Symptoms speak volumes
that nobody reads.
They give her the treatment
but not what she needs.

A doctor close at hand
who tries to understand
that sometimes pain is grief
is good beyond belief.

WISE SAYING: THERE'S A TIME AND A PLACE FOR EVERYTHING

"When can I howl?"
I'm waiting for the time to come
when I can let it out,
open my throat
and roar.
But I don't believe you when you say
"There's a time and a place,"
because I've never been there.
There's always some good reason
for being good,
for not disturbing the neighbours.
How much longer can you keep it up?
There's going to be a disaster
I can feel it coming
The world will fall about our ears!
We shall be destroyed!

"Now don't be silly, dear
This is all very dramatic.
You've got all these wild ideas,
Why don't you write a book about it?"

FINDING THE WORD FOR IT

When I told Colin
about the cold, left-over porridge
he said it was shit;
but that was the wrong colour.
Janet found a word for it
that fitted my feeling
that I couldn't swallow it,
couldn't stomach it.
Gloria thinks poems should be beautiful,
not disgusting, like some things are.
The way to stop child abuse
is to talk about it,
find an image,
find a word
and spit it out.

At school, I couldn't go out to play
until I had finished my mashed potato,
and Geoffrey was made to eat up
all his onions.

NIGHT SONG

I'm singing for a little girl
who's crying in the night
to tell her she need not be sad,
that everything's all right.

An evil monster is stood beside the bed
and this is what the evil monster said,
"You are sick you are mad
you are dangerous and bad!"
The child heard
every word
and thought it was true.
What can I do?

I'm talking to a little girl
who thinks she's in the wrong.
I'll comfort her and cheer her up
by singing her this song.

Little girl, little girl,
everything's all right;
the evil monster's gone, and we
are singing in the night.

THE DREAM OF THE BABY BEAR

Baby Bear came home and said
"Who's been sleeping in my bed?
Who ate all my porridge up?
Who's been drinking from my cup?
Who's been sitting on my chair?
Don't tell me! It's another bear!"

His parents said, "You mustn't growl,
you mustn't grunt, you mustn't howl.
We've got a little cub for you
and there is room enough for two.
You mustn't say it isn't fair
now you are big enough to share."

But Baby Bear began to scream
and said, "What happened to my dream?
I thought I was the only one,
but now - just look what you have done!"
Alas, his parents didn't care
and punished him, to his despair.

Oh, tell the tale of Goldilocks
with yellow hair and clean white socks
who came into the house of Bear
and ate and drank and slumbered there,
and tell us what we want to know
- that Goldilocks was MADE TO GO
so Baby Bear could reign supreme!
Oh, tell us for we need this dream.

THE CHILD IS INNOCENT

I learned it at my mother's knee,
this sooty black despair.
It never did belong to me -
I'll shake it from my hair!
I'll wash my hands of any wrong
and shake my little feet,
and with a new and happy song
go dancing down the street.
And if I see that sooty cloud
appear to block my way,
then I shall sing this song aloud
and turn aside to play.

A Love Song for my Feet

I love my pretty little feet.
I treat them very well;
I soak them in pink bubbles
that have a lovely smell,
I scrub them with a loofah,
I soften them with cream…
My feet say, "It's delightful!
It's better than a dream
to get so much attention!
It really is a treat!"
Dear little things! without them
I just wouldn't be complete.

AN INDEPENDENT CHILD

They can say what they like;
this child will never be
what they say he should be;
he will never be like them.
But he will wander away
into the woods on his own.
There he has his own den
and enjoys his own company.
Whatever he wants, he finds
or invents. He is the master,
with no one to show him how things are done,
no one to bring him up.
He is not lonely as you might think,
but free and independent,
only sad sometimes to realise
they do not know him,
and are not aware that they don't.

This child is very strong,
not needing to belong,
not needing to conform,
not needing any norm.
He is alone
and fully grown,
Nobody's person
but his own.

GROWING UP

What do we do now the witch is dead,
now the prince has come and gone,
and there is no Father Christmas?
Can we live without them?
Happily ever after?
or daren't we hope for that?

Our story isn't over;
there are monsters still
to confront.
Are we big enough to face them?
If we cry for help,
who will help us?

I wish, I wish
I still had a fairy godmother.

STRANGE THINGS

From walking up and down in the world
and going to and fro in it
I come to report to you
the things I have heard and seen.

I have seen trees standing on their heads,
I have heard frogs speaking.
You need not believe it, but listen.
I know a frog who lives in the desert.
He tells me strange things.
How can he live in the desert, you may ask.
You may well ask.
I cannot tell you.
You would have to speak to the frog yourself.
There is a way he can live in the desert,
there is a way.
Why does he live in the desert, you ask?
You may well ask,
and I can tell you.
He is looking for a princess.
But there are no princesses
in the desert, you say.
This is true.
He goes there in order to be quite sure
Of not finding one.
I told you, he tells me strange things.

GLORIA

Are you ready for Gloria?
She will be here soon.
Crazy girl in a yellow dress,
multicoloured beads,
singing, dancing,
spilling the beans;
the girl has flair,
sunshine in her hair…
Look out, look alive!
She will open all your cupboards,
leave nothing on your shelves
and ransack your heart,
your sweetie jar.
Look out, look alive!
Be ready for Gloria.
She's more than a match for you.

JOY

JOY is flowing like a river
JOY is dancing in the sun
JOY is working like a woman
Woman's work is never done.

JOY IS UNCONFINED

Like a sandboy
a bee in the clover
I bumbled
I fumbled...

Like a sandboy
a bee in the clover
I stumbled on JOY
and almost fell over.

SAFETY FIRST

You mustn't get too excited.
If you do, Alan will start to get nervous.
He is standing by
with a bucket of cold water,
and he will not hesitate to drench you.
That will dampen your ardour!
That will teach you to behave yourself!
He should have been a fireman,
always ready for emergencies,
ready to save you from yourself
and from the spark of life within you.
If you ring him up
he will say, "Can I help you?"
He will save you, he will help you
not to get too excited.

He keeps well away from Gloria.

EXCITEMENT

Gloria is very exciting
glittery and special
like a Christmas parcel
the child trembles to think of,
unable to sleep,
dying to touch
dying to know
fearful this joy
may be given to another
sister or brother...

Perhaps if the parcel were undressed,
the child would like the wrapping best.

WHEN

when the powerful let go of power
MAGIC!
when the sun gives its light to a flower
when the master comes down from his tower
when the tears fall like rain in a shower
the lady comes out of her bower
MAGIC!

Funny Friends

Now and then it seems to me
that here and there I have to be
up and down and inside out
down the tube and up the spout.

Here and now I must agree
it's really lovely to be me.

When the words dance on the page
I forget despair and rage
and then I have a lot of fun
with words that dance and play and run.

They run in such a funny way,
they lead my crazy thoughts astray.
They are my friends. I feel at ease
with such amusing friends as these.

Morning Headache

I lay in bed
reading a book
when I heard a noise.
I tried to ignore it
but it went on.
It was giving me a headache.

I went downstairs
"It's me," said the kitchen bin,
"crying out to be emptied,"
"and us," said the dishes,
"demanding to be washed."
"Wash me too," said the floor.
"Hoover me," said the carpet.
"Don't all talk at once.
No wonder I've got a headache!"

Suddenly from upstairs
I heard two piping voices.
My pen called, "Use me!"
A poem cried, "Write me!"
I flew upstairs to meet their needs
as the noise from below
rose in crescendo.

"You've this to do, and that to do!"
"I cannot do it now.
With this to do and that to do
I'll muddle through somehow.
I know there's this and that to do;
I can't do it today.

The thing about the housework is -
It will not go away.
A poem may."

The bath murmured, "Get in,"
Most invitingly,
While the crossword puzzle
muttered in the corner.
I solved it right in the bubbles.
"That's right.
Forget all about me!"
my headache hissed,
dissolving in the steam.

ITCHY EYES

We breathe to live, and yet with every breath
we breathe in lead and benzine, cancer, death.
We eat and drink destruction every day.
We have to try to find another way.
My eyes swell up, enraged at what they see;
the doctor says, "It's just an allergy."
I'm trying to relax and simply live.
Why am I so intense and sensitive?
I drop in drops and swallow all my pills,
take long weekends away from city ills.
I must be odd, I must be strange,
for voices in my head cry, "Things must change!"
I write it down, and find to my surprise
that everyone agrees, and thinks it wise
to clean the air, the water and the food.
They do not think me odd or mad or rude.
"Oh no," they say, "you're right, it isn't funny.
But put it right? Well, that would cost us money."

WHO? WHY? HOW?

"Who is this woman
with her head held high?
For pride like that
she deserves to die!
Who is this woman?
How does she dare...?
She should be ashamed -
but she just doesn't care.
She's really changed,
I don't know how.
She's pleasing herself
and enjoying it now.
So scared and shy,
she used to be.
What happened?"
"Well, it's the therapy!"

Virginia Harrison

Fat, Forty and Feeling Good

'Fat' what's that?
'Thin' is a sin.
Round and robust
Is an absolute must.
The folds of the skin
Keep everything in.
More flesh on the face
For a smile to embrace.
Full and fickle
More body to tickle.
Forcing a giggle
more bottom to wiggle,
Like Play-Doh to mould
Big and bold
'Fat' what's that?
Better than 'flat'.

HOMELESS

Invisible to the world that goes on around
Perched upon the pavement,
Cocooned in a sleeping bag of holes
Or cramped in a cardboard box upon the ground

Faces conceal youthfulness
As the grime of the streets
Penetrates exposed skin
Like pawns in a game of chess

My search reveals plenty
Of homeless people but
Not the one I wish to find
The one originating from gentry

My feet throb within my shoes
A consequence of pounding on pavements,
Hours of brisk walking,
Pushing through queues.

The posher part of town
Reveals a soul,
Away from others
Wearing a combination of gowns

The face strikes a chord of familiarisation
A mother's recognition
I place a Tupperware of home-cooked food and a flask of tea
At his feet knowing there would be no reconciliation
I glance behind
As I walk away

But the offerings remain in situ
I have to be grateful for my find

Days, weeks and months pass by
The same ritual taking place
But with no acknowledgement
As I leave my son, I cry

Then an action to suggest
Appeasement
I notice the flask of hot tea
Cradled tight to his chest

A thumb is raised
A smile spreads across his face
I don't pretend to understand
But at that moment my heart is ablaze

STEPHEN STOP IT

My name is Stephen Stoppit
Or so I was led to believe
Until the day I started school
And was promptly asked to leave.

"Stephen STOP IT," Mum would shout
As I ate worms and slugs
"Stephen STOP IT," Mum would scream
As I pulled the wings off bugs.

Now my teacher tells me
I must be Stephen Raine
As that's what's on the register
You'd think Mum would know my name.

No more does Mum shout, "STOP IT"
Instead, it's, "Stephen you're a PAIN!"
Now I understand
That must be my real name.

Next day at school I declared
"Miss, I'm not Stephen Raine"
"Please change your register to read"
"Stephen.......PAYNE"

THE DISAPPEARING ACT

Big socks or little socks
It doesn't really matter
They go in together
And then they seem to scatter.

Washing comes to an end
I peer into the drum
Reach in and pull out lots of clothes
But now two socks are one.

I've many well-worn footwear
But none of them are pairs.
I keep them neatly folded
In drawers, upon the stairs.

I thought my machine was eating them
So I swapped it for another.
But no, the same thing happens
I always lose the brother

NO matter how I twist or tie
Each item to its partner
They separate when out of view
The remaining one the martyr.

This has gone on for many years
The mystery still unsolved
I've resorted now to hand-washing
Where I can get involved.

THE NATIVITY

You grimace and wince with so much pain
Knowing you must say "No" again.
"No," you stammer despite their plea.
Your heart pounding at the thought of your deed.
You suddenly shout, "Alright, I have a room at the back."
The teacher's glare, her expression so black.
"NO NO NO," she stresses
"I've told you before
"You've no room at the inn when they knock at the door."
"But, Miss, she's with child
I've been taught to be kind
I'm sure the audience will not mind."
A sigh of concern as she tries to explain
"We're re-enacting the Bible".
They start rehearsing again.

The parents arrive and take their seats.
As the music starts, there's much tapping of feet.
This time when approached,
the innkeeper says, "No,"
stressing that no room means they must go.
As they take their leave,
the innkeeper looks with despair,
at his teacher smiling, sat on her chair.
The silence interrupted,
he raises his voice,
"No room at the inn, but some tea
and cakes of your choice."

WHAT, WHO, WHY?

I ask you a question
"What's wrong, Mum?"
You don't answer but
Your eyes reveal all,
as a lonely tear
Courses through the wrinkles
On your face.
Balancing for a brief moment on your lips
Until sucked within, through your sobbing.
I clasp your hand tightly for fear
Of losing you.
The next day you ask me a question
"Who are you?"
I shed many more tears than you.
They follow the same route
as yours but across my own face
While I mouth the words
"Goodbye, Mum"

WILD THING

How you drag me from my home
Clasping tight upon my coat
Tugging it free from my shoulders,
To reveal the flesh upon my bone.

How you ruffle my hair
and claw at my face
until red weal marks appear
replacing a complexion that was once fair

No matter how I try
To push against your strength
Or use an umbrella as weaponry
You still force me to cry

Every attempt is made
To stop me fleeing to another
Obstacles strewn across my path
As a barricade

I know your intentions are well-meant
Such as making others strong and being
Instrumental in the ecology of plants
But I find your forcefulness a torment.

My heart yearns for love and desire
not destruction
Sensual caressing of my skin
Like a ballet of golden samphire
Tenderness that provides security
As I disrobe and expose my flesh

In the privacy of the moment
I offer up my love in its entirety

Your rasping can still be heard
As you watch over me from a distance
Calmer than before, but
you remain undeterred

You have lost my heart to another
You drove me away
With your arrogance and brashness
Gale force wind tussles exchanged for a sunshine lover

ALL IN A DAY'S WORK

M aggie sighed deeply as her car finally reached the end of the estate. Just as she was about to give up, she noticed an elderly lady peering over the garden wall. "Excuse me," she shouted from her car window.

The staunch figure tried to appear startled, wiping her mottled hands on her apron. She walked towards the car.

"Can you direct me to Country Cottage? A gentleman called Matthew Rathbone lives there." Maggie said.

"Yes, my dear," came the reply in an accent that sounded pretentious, like she was trying to impress. "It's at the other end of the estate. The last house set back from the road just after passing the post box."

Maggie was just about to say thank you and continue on her way when the lady broke into further conversation.

"Funny chap." She continued as she rested her hands on the open window, preventing Maggie from driving away. "Seventy-eight, and he lives with his brother, I believe. He keeps himself to himself. Never smiles. We only see him when he goes to tend to his sheep, which he keeps in a field at the other side of the town. Gave his house the silly name of Country Cottage because he likes to think he is still living in the country. Hates towns. When we do see him, he only nods his head." She gave a quick demonstration with a nod of her own head. "We don't like not knowing who is living on our estate. We call him Ratty Matty."

Maggie quickly got in a "thank you" and gently wound her window up, forcing the neighbour to remove her hands and cut the conversation short. She was already late for her appointment.

Driving slowly back through the housing estate in the direction she had come, she caught sight of the post box and saw a painted wooden gate half opened, with a tarnished brass plate on it. Perhaps he had visitors or maybe it would not shut fully. The house looked very run down. Putting the car into neutral, she pulled the handbrake on tight for fear that it might lunge off down the hill, leaving her at the mercy of Mr Rathbone and his brother.

She knocked at the door. A crooked figure emerged, huddled over a walking stick. His arm was embedded in a plaster cast up to his shoulder, and his neck was encased in a surgical collar. Her own appearance was immaculate, dressed in social service uniform, beneath a full-length navy blue wool coat.

In contrast, the old man was clothed in torn trousers and a misshapen grey jumper. Rough stubble hid any sign of a smile, and what little hair he had left clung to his skull as if fearful of abduction. Maggie immediately felt guilty for judging him on first appearances, since it would be very difficult for him to shave and wash in his present condition.

"Mr Rathbone?" she asked

"Who wants to know?" he wheezed.

"I'm your home help, Maggie," she replied taking her coat off as she gently eased her way through the door.

"Don't take your coat off, lassie. We're off out," was his reply, ushering her back out of the door towards the car. "I need you to take me down to the sheep. They need feeding."

Somehow, his abrupt manner and pleading eyes made her warm to him. "Well, really Mr Rathbone, I'm a home help," she said, emphasising the *home*. "and as such I help in the home."

"Aah, well I'll extend your duties then," he replied.

Although she wanted to argue, she felt sympathetic to his predicament and proceeded towards the car. She knew his request was against regulations but decided there was no harm in chauffeuring him to his field on this one occasion.

"Where is your brother? Can he not help?" she questioned.

"My brother?" he looked puzzled, and then he said, "Oh, my brother won't work."

Totally confused by this answer she continued on her way.

Perhaps his brother was senile and unable to carry out farming duties, or perhaps he was just lazy, she thought.

"STOP. We're here," came a shriek from her occupant as he tapped her on the shoulder. "These are my sheep."

He pointed to a mass of wool huddled together. "You'll find the hay in the barn over there. Drag a bale into that feeder. That should keep them going for a while. Oh, and there's a tap at the back of the barn with a hose pipe attached. Fill up the trough. There's a good lassie."

Disbelieving she turned to face him. "I can't feed your sheep. I'm a home help, and I'm not dressed for rummaging in fields and barns," she retorted.

"Aye a very pretty lass, but it were a bit silly not putting wellies on. Now git!"

Why she ventured out of the car and carried out his demands, she did not know. Perhaps it was the sight of him looking uncomfortably constrained.

As she struggled, out of breath, with a bale of hay, she could hear constant instructions being shouted from the car window. Unable to hear clearly from where she was standing, she continued with her task as best she could, thinking all the time how lucky he was that she was doing this for him anyway. If she were caught feeding sheep, she would certainly face disciplinary action as it was bound to contravene all the health and safety rules.

As she hauled the bale of hay into the feeder, she felt something caress her bottom and then a sudden force pushed her forward against the feeder and caused the heels on her shoes to sink into the mud.

"Well, really, Mr Rathbone! I will not stand for that kind of behaviour," she said as she turned around, but Mr Rathbone was still sitting in the car. Her abusers were the sheep, anxious to get to the food. She was relieved Mr Rathbone had not heard her accusations. "Give me a chance to get it in the feeder, then it's all yours," she said to the sheep, but they continued to nudge her out of the way.

As she attempted to walk away, she realised her heels were stuck fast. As she pulled and pulled the heel of one of her shoes broke off. "Damn," she shouted as she flung her shoes across the field. She emerged from the field covered in hay, mud up to her ankles, torn stockings and shoeless.

Back in the more familiar surroundings of her car, she sat quietly, holding back the tears.

"You're a good lass," came the comforting words from her passenger. "I heard you talking to them. I think they like you. A word of advice though: next time, don't turn your back on them and then you'll see if they are going to head-butt you and you can move out of the way. Never mind, you did well. A natural." Mr Rathbone smiled for the first time since their meeting, but all Maggie could manage in return was a menacing glance.

Maggie started the car. The journey back to the housing estate was grim. Not a word spoken. Mr Rathbone struggled out of the car whilst inviting her in for a cup of coffee as a reward for her good deed. Totally exhausted, she politely declined the offer. She did not have enough energy to make conversation with Mr Rathbone and his brother.

Maggie was anxious to dowse her body in herbal bliss, ridding herself of the lingering stomach-wrenching farmyard odours.

"I'll pop in tomorrow to check how you are," she said. "But I can't be feeding your sheep every day. I need to help with your domestic needs."

"I ain't got no domestic needs," he grumbled.

Maggie knew it was useless arguing. She would have to be more diplomatic tomorrow. The next day, she approached the house, clad in casual clothing and mindful that her wellies were stashed in the boot of the car, just in case Mr Rathbone had organised more manual work for her to perform.

She knocked at the door, but no-one answered. She knocked louder but still silence.

"You won't get an answer. He's not there," came a voice from the roadside. Glancing round, she recognised the speaker as the lady she had met yesterday, who had directed her to the house in the first place.

"Do you know when he will be back?" she asked. "He won't. He's dead. Pneumonia, I believe."

She felt the blood surge from her face and stammered, "But he was fine yesterday. A bit chesty maybe, but nothing serious."

"Well, he's dead now." Came the blunt reply

"Where's his brother?" Maggie asked.

"I don't know. I never met his brother. I just know the ambulance came in the night. I don't like to pry into other people's business," She replied unconvincingly.

Maggie did not stay to hear anymore. As she passed the field of sheep, she slowed her vehicle as a mark of respect, wondering who would look after them now. Her first thought was that perhaps she could put out enough feed to last until the arrangements were made, but her legs were shaking uncontrollably. She would never have enough strength to lift the bale of hay today.

Sitting silently at her desk, she could feel tears welling up in her eyes. She felt immensely guilty that she had been so annoyed at carrying out such a simple task as feeding sheep. How rude she had been to drive off, refusing his kind offer of refreshments. Even when she had got home, she had scrubbed her body, cursing, until sores had appeared, leaving her skin looking like the inside of a pomegranate.

Her solitude was broken by a grey-haired, well-dressed gentleman carrying a suitcase.

"Maggie Thomas?" he queried.

"Yes."

"I believe you knew Mr Rathbone of Country Cottage?" he said.

"Well, I'd hardly say knew... more... met him once," she replied, dabbing her eyes with a scrunched-up paper hanky that had fallen victim to her anger.

"I found this note," he said, offering her a crumpled piece of paper.

She started to read it. It read, 'I'm tired and not feeling too well. If anything should happen to me, I want that pretty social services lassie Maggie to have my brother as a thank you for all her help. The kind of help she gave me was what I needed. Not ironing, washing and other stuff. My sheep are the most important thing to me, and Maggie did as I asked with very little complaint. She even talked to them as she fed them, which shows me she is a warm, caring person.'

With disbelief, she looked up into the gentleman's eyes and said, "You must be Mr Rathbone's brother." Not waiting for an answer, she tried to think how she was going to cope with looking after a senile, lazy old man whilst continuing to work. Suddenly, she realised she was being self-centred again. It was the least she could do until some satisfactory alternative arrangements could be made.

"Oh no, miss," he answered politely. "I'm Mr Craven from Craven & Simpkin solicitors. This is Mr Rathbone's brother." In an instant, he had lifted the suitcase onto the desk, forcing open the clasps to reveal a printer. The make, a Brother.

"I don't understand?" she said.

Mr Craven sighed. "I was a good friend of Matthew's. He missed his home in the country, and I once suggested that he should write about his life to help him come to terms with his move. He found it extremely difficult to write in long hand with his arthritis, so I bought him a laptop and printer and booked him onto a course in the local community centre. I thought it would be good for him to get out of the house and meet other people. It wasn't for him. He gave the laptop away years ago, but he kept the printer even though he had no means of using it."

Maggie's face reddened with embarrassment as she connected the printer to her own laptop and tried it out.

Her printed words read, "I am sorry about the misunderstanding and only too glad to have been of help. Rest in peace, and thank you.

I'll treasure this gift forever."

An Unexpected Visitor

I noticed him again, standing looking up at the bedroom window. Every day this week, he had been waiting and watching. He hadn't seen me, peering behind the curtains. It didn't matter what the weather was like. He would always be there. Sometimes he would be grinning to himself as if someone had shared a very funny joke with him. Yet, at other times, I am sure I saw him discretely dabbing his eyes with a freshly laundered handkerchief.

Why did I let him in? I know why. He wore a freshly pressed business suit and shiny tan-coloured brogue shoes. He looked so charming and I was curious. It had taken me several attempts to finally pluck up the courage to open the front door and ask him inside. I didn't want to appear intrusive, but, like I said, I was curious.

We made a connection right from the start. The image of him sitting in front of the coal fire, resting his feet on the chipped emerald green marble hearth, lingered in my memory.

I remember I encouraged him to take his shoes off to allow him to dry his feet. The rain had been relentless and his shoes had soaked up all the moisture. The tan-colour was replaced by soggy brown water marks. I did so hope the stains were not permanent. He took little persuading and showed no embarrassment whatsoever when he noticed me glancing at his mismatched socks. I am not entirely sure whether they were odd socks or whether one of them had faded in the wash. Either way, he no longer had the appearance of a professional person. He looked more like a scruffy young boy waiting for his mum to bring him his supper.

He sat comfortably, drinking tea and praising me on my cooking skills, as he ate the ginger cake that I had baked that morning. I tried to give him as much information about his grandfather as I could, but it was a long time ago, and I had only been a neighbour, not family. We both laughed when I told him about the time that his grandmother, Audrey, brought home a newborn lamb, convinced that it was her pet dog, and his grandfather had screamed at her in the street, saying that she was a crazy lady. Audrey seemed not to care and was delighted that he considered her a "lady". The farmer had come running down the street, furious. Audrey had only jumped over a dry-stone wall and scooped the lamb up in her arms and scurried away. It didn't take long to return the lamb to its rightful owner and diffuse the situation.

It was sad, really, that Audrey spent so much time trapped in a world within her own mind. She meant no harm to anyone and she seemed perfectly happy. Even though I remember his grandfather being impatient with Audrey on many occasions, I didn't want to give the impression that they had an unhappy marriage, so I conveniently missed out some details. He scribbled down everything I said on a pad that he had taken out of his jacket pocket, making reference notes to the family tree that he had drawn on the front page. The excitement was evident in his face as dates and events slotted together.

He suddenly stopped writing and apologised profusely for not even asking my name. His eyes lit up when I told him that I was called Denise. Evidently, I have the same name as his sister.

Once he had finished his tea and cake, I showed him around my house, knowing that it would be identical to the one next door where his grandparents had lived. He told me about some photographs he had at home, showing his ancestors enjoying a summer drink in the garden. They were obviously well-off because he remembers his parents making references to afternoons playing polo. I did think it peculiar that people from a very affluent background would choose to live in this area, but then some people prefer to disguise their true wealth. Not that there is anything wrong with this area.

I remember thinking what a shame it was that he had come all this way and Simon and Beverley, my next-door neighbours, were out at work. It would have been so much more interesting for him to go around the actual family home. They rarely got in from work until gone 6pm and he explained that he had to leave by four at the latest as it was his turn to pick his son up from the after-school club. He seemed a little irritated that he would have to come back another day.

I deduced from his comment about it being his turn to do the school run that he must be separated or divorced from his wife. He looked so kind, and he was very attractive. It puzzled me why his wife would decide to separate from him. Some people were never satisfied.

Why did next door have to be out at work? It seemed such a shame that he would have to come back to visit the actual ancestral home, but at least it would give me an opportunity to speak to him again and learn some more about his son.

I gave him my telephone number so that he could ring and let me know when he would next be in the area, but suggested he didn't make it a Tuesday as I went to the church coffee morning and then on to friends for lunch. I agreed that once he phoned me, I would let Simon and Beverley know when to expect him so that they could arrange to be in. I didn't feel it was right to give him their phone number without their permission.

How stupid I had been.

The police asked me if I knew who could have broken into my home while I was out, but somehow, I couldn't bring myself to mention him. If I had, they would have gone back to the station saying things like "when will these old people learn?".

I should have known better because it's true, you do always hear it on television. "A trickster conned a VULNERABLE person."

That's what they call OLD people like me. Implying we are stupid. I had been stupid, though.

I bet he isn't even called John Swinton. John Swindler, more like. No, it's better that I get on with my life and just be a bit more careful in future. I can't even let on to anyone at church because I know they will gossip about how I'm too trusting. The only person I did tell was my friend Moira, and then, as soon as I had done it, I wished I hadn't.

I've known Moira for twenty years, and she has been a good friend, but I can hear her now, telling me, in her condescending manner, how I had better learn from this and not to punish myself too much as it's fortunate that I don't have anything of value.

Not like her, who has a collection of the most expensive jewels anyone can imagine, and she always keeps plenty of cash in her house in case of emergencies. That's wicked of me to say that because the only person who has telephoned to see if I'm alright is Moira, so maybe she isn't all that bad.

My thoughts were disturbed by the doorbell ringing.

"Hi, Denise."

"Oh, hi, Moira. I really appreciate you walking to the coffee morning with me. I'm still a bit shaken up after the robbery. Every time I go out, I keep having to go back to check the door is locked, even though I know I always lock it."

"How awful. Do the police know who did it?" asked Moira

"No. Probably just some lad who chanced his luck," I responded guiltily.

Moira gave me a hug and, like normal, bounded into conversation.

"Never mind. The things they took probably aren't worth a lot. Except perhaps sentimental value, I mean. Anyway, it's good to see you back at the coffee mornings and I have some fantastic news. Earlier on, a young man knocked on my door and evidently, he is tracing his family tree and one of his ancestors actually lived in my house. We got talking for ages, and I nearly missed the bus to get here. I explained that I had to go to the coffee morning and that I wouldn't be home till about 3 o'clock, so he is coming back then to finish where we left off. I'll have to ring you tomorrow and let you know how I get on."

"Oh, Moira, please be careful," I said, trying not to give anything away, but I could hear my own voice trembling. "I know. Why don't we give the coffee morning a miss and go back to your place for coffee instead?" I said, trying to sound a little bit more convincing and less worried.

"Honestly, Denise, I understand your concern, but not everyone is out to rob people. Like you said, it was probably just some young lad trying his luck. Get your coat or we'll be late."

ME AND PADDY O'NEILL

T he anxiety was too much. Simon had laid awake in bed for two hours or more, just watching the second hand moving around the clock, waiting. Waiting for a reasonable hour when he could emerge without causing annoyance to the rest of the household.

Daylight was just beginning to shine through the gap in the curtains, making shadows on the second-hand music centre placed on top of the chest of drawers. That was his cue. He swung his legs out of bed and raced toward the wardrobe. Flinging the doors open wide, he pulled on a bright green t-shirt and pale blue trousers. Meanwhile, he hunted for a pair of socks that looked vaguely similar. Clothes were strewn all over the floor as a result of his search. He couldn't waste any more time looking for shoes, so he decided upon slippers, which were close by. No-one would see him anyway at such an early hour of the morning, apart from his closest friend, Paddy O'Neill, and Paddy was always non-judgemental. The last item of clothing would be his imitation leather jacket.

Within minutes, he was at Paddy's bedside, shaking him urgently and dragging him out of bed. "Come on, Paddy. Wake up. You can be the first person to see my main birthday present." Simon helped Paddy get dressed, and they made their way, in silence, down the stairs to the back door.

Although Simon knew he was getting a bike, he had never expected anything quite so enormous and beautiful. The bike had an azure blue frame and bold black handlebars with star-shaped spoke wheels that looked quite menacing.

"It's a good job I'm not married or got a girlfriend," he whispered. "There's no way girls would want a ride on this. They would be too frightened of the speed it can go."

He remembered how his parents had often talked about this day and how he must wear the appropriate headgear and take lessons to ride it properly. A definite sign of their age. Well, he had the helmet, albeit a tight fit, but the lessons would have to wait because he couldn't arrange anything at this time of the morning.

Running his hands over the seat and handlebars, he grinned at Paddy. Paddy still looked very sleepy, but Simon knew he was just as excited. Legs placed either side and their bottoms firmly in the seat, Simon slowly manoeuvred the bike backwards and forwards to get a feel for the weight and size. It was such a comfortable riding position, but it did seem a long way down to the ground.

With some difficulty turning the bike around, they were eventually facing the direction they wanted to go in. Unfortunately, a few plants that overhung onto the drive had been decapitated in the process, but with the past few days' intense heat and hosepipe ban, they had been fading fast anyway. Nevertheless, Simon used his feet to bury the evidence beneath the soil while the remaining flowers appeared to nod their heads with disapproval in the gentle breeze.

"Right, Paddy. We had better not go far. We'll just go to the end of the farm lane and collect the morning milk, and then after breakfast, we will go a bit further. On the way back, we can swap places if you like, but I will still control it; after all it is my birthday present. The milk can slide in the front of my jacket for now, but perhaps you could get me some panniers as a belated birthday present."

Paddy wasn't very good at remembering vital dates and certainly lacked imagination when it came to having ideas about presents, but Simon didn't mind. Somehow, it made him feel all the more important, being the brains behind the duo.

The bike glided along the lane, picking up speed as it approached a slight decline. Trees lined the edge as if on an inspection parade, with their damp leaves glistening in the sunlight, exposing protruding veins that were lighter in colour.

Panicking at the change of speed, Simon threw his feet off the supports and onto the ground to try to slow the vehicle. He forgot it had brakes. A sharp burning sensation could be felt biting through his slippers. Both lads wobbled from side to side as he tried to maintain the weight of the bike and stop it from falling. The last thing he wanted to do was to scratch it on his first ride out. Simon could see the displeasure on Paddy's face and was pleased that Paddy refrained from scolding him.

This did not deter him from his task, even though it took him some time before he plucked up the courage to restart and try again.

To build up his confidence, Simon tried leaning from left to right and found he could shift his body weight accordingly to balance the weight of the bike. He did not need such a tight grip on the handlebars, and he could even take one hand off completely.

Feeling much more confident, he longed to go beyond the lane end, but controlled the urge to do so. Slowing the bike down, he approached his target and dismounted. He heaved the vehicle onto its stand. As he bent down to collect the milk, he noticed how the blue of the bike was glistening in the sunlight. He still could not believe it belonged to him.

The shrieks of a woman brought him back to reality. He recognised the verbal tones, closely followed by a vision of his mother with a dressing gown draped over her shoulders.

"Stop!" she shouted. "What on earth are you doing?" she asked without waiting for an answer. "NEVER NEVER go out without me knowing!"

Tears welled up in Simon's eyes. His mother never normally behaved like this.

He stuttered. "I'm six today. You've got to trust me. Me and Paddy were only collecting the milk for breakfast."

His mother could see the child's sadness as he clutched Paddy, his teddy bear, in one hand and a pint of milk in the other. It was obvious he had thought she would be so proud of his achievement, and instead, her calmness had splintered.

Turning the bike around to face the direction of the farmhouse, she tried to explain her concern and how she thought he was going to try the bike out on the road. She lifted him and Paddy O'Neill back onto the bike and kissed his cheek.

Taking the milk bottle from him, she agreed to race him home. Simon did not wait for her to count to three but pedalled as fast as he could, shrieking with delight. The squeals of laughter alerted his father, who emerged from the farmhouse to see his son enjoying his present.

Once they reached the house, his mother promised faithfully that after breakfast, he could ride his new pushbike all the way to the park, on one condition that she go with him. Well, it was a start. Maybe tomorrow, when he was older, he could go by himself.

THE WHITE LADY

N ow, children, I want you to help Mrs Goldsborough, your
mother's new nurse, as much as possible," said Derek
Masters. "Meanwhile, I will help the removal firm to unpack our
boxes."

"I think the best thing we could do is keep out of Dad's way by
exploring in the garden," said Julie, the eldest daughter.

"What a good idea!" came Derek's reply.

"Come on everyone, let's go," said Julie as she bent down to pick
up Jamie who was trying to shuffle along on his bottom but found his
nappy too restrictive.

"I'd much rather stop in the house and play marbles," Simon
moaned.

"Julie's in charge," said the twins in unison.

All the children trudged outside, following Julie as she carried
Jamie.

"Look, I only suggested coming outside so that I could talk to you
all. I read a newspaper article yesterday suggesting that this house is
haunted by a lady in white. It said she is often seen strolling around
the chapel further down the lane, crying and saying she is sorry. I
thought it might be fun if we watched for her one night."

Charlotte and Beatrice, the ten-year-old twins also thought it
would be fun, but Susan had reservations.

"What if she makes us go with her to heaven?" said Susan. "I'm
only eight and I don't want to go to heaven yet."

"I'm only six," said Simon "but I don't mind just visiting heaven."

"Don't be silly," Julie mocked. "You don't go to heaven until
you're dead. We'll just follow her and see what she does and where
she goes. We won't let her see us."

They all agreed that Julie would wake them up at 3am, and they
would make their way to the library next to their mother's ground-
floor room in the west wing to wait for the white lady to appear. This

was the area of the house where sightings had been reported.

Julie lay awake, waiting for the grandfather clock to chime. On the third strike, she swung her legs out of bed, pulled some clothes on top of her pyjamas and hurried to the twins' room. Charlotte and Beatrice were already waiting. Susan took longer to wake and insisted on taking her teddy bear with her. Simon refused to go. He was much too tired and threatened to scream unless they let him sleep. The four of them crept onto the landing and made their way to the library.

They snuggled down behind a thick red velvet curtain and waited. Their breathing sounded as if it was getting louder. It wasn't long before the air turned very cold and the sound of weeping could be heard. Susan gasped in horror and dropped her teddy. Julie clasped her hand over Susan's mouth to stop her from screaming and they all peered around the curtain. Pacing up and down was a lady dressed in a lace gown. She suddenly turned and raced out of the library into the corridor and went towards the pantry. The children followed, with Julie taking the lead. As the lady in white reached the pantry door, she seemed to disappear. Julie opened the door and turned on the light, but there was nothing to be seen. The other three children were huddled together with fright. As they turned around, they saw a large figure looming over them and all four children screamed.

"What on earth is going on?" their father shouted. "Julie, explain yourself."

"Father, we were following the white lady. You know the ghost that everyone says haunts this house?"

"Utter rubbish," he snarled, "and at 15, I would expect you to know better than to involve your sisters in a silly game. Now back to bed, everyone."

"But, Dad."

"No buts Julie. Bed now, all of you!"

As Julie began to make her way back, she felt the flagstone underfoot move. She stopped and stood on it again just to make sure and was about to tell her father but thought better of it. She would tell him in the morning when he was in a better mood.

The following day, Derek decided to take all the family to the seaside, but when he went to Julie's room she complained of a bad stomach.

"I'll stay in bed if you don't mind," she said

"Are you sure you'll be alright on your own?"

"Yes, I'm sure."

"I shouldn't wonder that you haven't caught a chill with your late-night wanderings," he chuntered.

Julie watched from her bedroom window as the children clambered into the car and the nurse lifted her mother from the wheelchair into the passenger seat. Her father forced the boot shut and settled in the driver's seat. The car slowly rolled down the drive. That was Julie's cue. She dressed and headed towards the pantry. Food was not her aim. She walked up and down the corridor near the pantry, looking for the loose flagstone. She found it. Easing her fingers down the sides, she pulled at it and after much heaving, it lifted out of position. There seemed to be a tunnel below.

She ran to the front door and took a torch from the cupboard, then, with trepidation, she switched it on and made her way back to the tunnel entrance. Clasping the torch tight, she jumped down into the hole and started walking. It was dark, damp and very eerie. She tried to visualise in which direction she was walking, but she lost track as the tunnel seemed to weave from left to right and back again. After some time, she came to a dead end. She tried pushing on the walls around her to find a way out, but nothing. Reluctantly, she turned around and headed back the way she had come, but as she did so she thought she heard footsteps above her. She stopped to listen. The footsteps seemed to echo all around as if there was a building above, yet she was sure she had walked some distance, which would mean that it couldn't be their home, Hatterstone Hall.

The footsteps stopped and Julie reached above her. The earth crumbled away to reveal a wooden shaft. She pushed up as hard as she could, and the wood slats moved slowly. She reached up and put her torch on the ground above and peered out. She was looking up into the chapel. There, she saw a priest praying near the altar. Quickly, she eased the wood slats back into position and hurried through the tunnel towards home, stumbling as she went. She had left her torch on the chapel floor, but it was too risky to go back for it.

When Julie reached the other end, she could see the comforting glow from the hall light. Gently, she climbed onto safe ground, replaced the flagstone and went to her room to tidy herself up. She slid into bed and waited for the family's return.

The next night, Julie decided not to involve the others, but she was still anxious to find out who the white lady was. This time, she would wait at the chapel in the lane as she was sure that the lady must have slid into the tunnel and was probably heading for the chapel.

When the hall clock struck 3am, Julie dressed and made her way outside, heading towards the chapel. As it came into view, she could see the lights on. Peering through the open door, she saw the priest kneeling at the tunnel entrance, waiting for someone.

The wood floor moved and the priest lunged backward as the white lady floated out of the tunnel sobbing frantically. She seemed to stare straight at the priest and chanted,

"I'm so sorry. Oh so sorry."

The priest shouted, "Lizzy I'm OK. Trouble yourself no more. Be at peace. Please be at peace. You are forgiven."

He lifted his hand and the lady faded away.

Julie had not realised that she had slowly been walking towards the priest, who suddenly became aware of her presence. He swung around, nervous of how much Julie had seen.

"Hello," said Julie, "who are you and who was that lady?"

"I'm Father Green and that lady is my sister."

"Is she a ghost?" asked Julie, her voice shaking.

"She will trouble us no more," he replied. "Many years ago, I wanted to become a priest, but the villagers were wicked and wanted to hurt me because they did not understand and thought that worshipping my god was evil. I was afraid, so I hid in the tunnel. They turned on my sister, saying she was a witch, and they tortured her, so she tried to save herself by telling them where to find me. I could hear them coming after me so I ran and hid in Hatterstone Hall. My sister could not rest in peace, knowing she had betrayed me. Now I think she knows I have forgiven her and, like I said, she will no longer trouble you. Are you from the family who have just moved into Hatterstone Hall?"

"Yes," came Julie's reply

"I trust your family don't know where you are?"

"No, I sneaked out," said Julie, looking ashamed.

"Your family will worry. Let me walk you home and I will speak with your father about getting the tunnel secured. You need to concentrate on getting your mother well again."

Father Green led Julie out of the chapel into daybreak and headed towards Hatterstone Hall, chatting as they walked along the lane.

Julie's father was waiting in the doorway with a worried expression on his face. As Julie came into view, he hurried down the drive and hugged her with relief, but nevertheless determined to show his authority he shouted, "Where have you been? I have been worried sick!"

"I was looking for the white lady."

"Not that nonsense again," said Derek.

"It's not nonsense. She went through the tunnel to the chapel to apologise to Father Green and…"

"Who's Father Green?" interrupted her father.

"The chapel priest and he's walked me home," she said as she turned around to introduce him. But no-one was there.

"Come on, we need to get you into bed," her father said in a mellow voice. "I will call a doctor in the morning. You really are ill. You have obviously been hallucinating."

147

JO LONG

This is Goodbye

You pulled me in, tucking me in your pocket,
Held me there, tight, caught in your locket.

Day in day out, back and forth,
Laughs, worries, tears, we had them all.

Then someone new came into sight,
Someone you thought would be better in your life.

I thought you were busy getting on
You were, but with another one.

I stood in your shadow, constant fake smile,
Saying nothing, just waiting and watching awhile.

Knowing deep down something wasn't right,
Not brave enough to say or cause upset outright.

Maybe it was all in my head, I thought,
(What an idea my mind had bought.)

I wore a bright mask of happiness and light,
I stepped back more and more, almost out of sight.

Then a lightbulb moment confirmed what I thought,
You'd gone swimming elsewhere, someone else you'd caught.

Those new to your voice, new to listen, laugh and weep,
Those with influence, kudos, the benefits you could reap.

My pride bruised and battered in a heap on the floor
I retreated, you didn't notice, back to where I was before.

I flayed in the wind, not knowing where to turn,
You'd cut off everything, all my bridges you'd burned.

You never looked back as in limbo I found
Nothing solid under my feet, no firm ground.

Bereft and lost, like a child alone at sea,
Worst of all, thinking it was all down to me.

Time passed as I watched silently from the wings
Adding unsuspecting casualties and all they would bring.

My sealed lips never spoke a word until questions asked
Then the truth was told, out in the open, and I removed my mask.

I was honest, I know the truth, I've seen it again and again
The same pattern repeated for your own personal gain.

And then your attempted return (which I'll never understand why)
Sticky sweet, assuming, apologies bone dry.

An expectation of shouts of joy, trumpets and red carpet
That isn't how we work, you know, so don't be so downhearted.

No screams of delight, no special treatment given,
If you want to earn your place, it's better to be forgiven.

This time it was you left floating, feeling for the edge,
No tether to keep you close, out there on the ledge.

I'll never relish your hurt or the tears that flowed,
But I'll never put a hand out either, that door is definitely closed.

My wounds have healed, I know now where I stand
Close to those I can fully trust, others at the distance of a hand.

I thank you for the lesson, for helping me to grow
To understand what I truly need, and when I can say no.

No doubt you'll continue through life oblivious to your destruction,
Repeating the same behaviour, just in various levels of fluxion,

I'm waving you goodbye and I'll always wish you well
I hope one day you settle but no longer will I dwell,
With these words from my heart it's finally farewell.

LOVE EARTHLY AND ABOVE

A love-filled heart knows no bounds,
Engorged overflowing, sees beauty all around.

Earthly love with all its riches
Solid, grounded, delights, bewitches.

Like a drug it seeps and grows,
Creating blindness to all that's known.

The need to be close can't be described,
The desire to be skin inside.

Pull close the face for a kiss,
Arms and legs wrapped, attention for only this.

Heavenly face vague, eyes glancing down,
To this earthly love will never be bound.

It seeks more celestial satisfaction,
A meeting of spirits without physical faction.

And so presents the double-edged sword,
One dedicated to carnal love with one in disaccord.

The masks of deceit and promise lie
At their feet, slid from faces high.

Fleeting passion mistaken for devotion,
On one part true, the other pure deception.

Unmoved by the kiss, attention distracted,

Oblivious to the pain that is attracted.

The tormented soul with a heart that bleeds
For affection, out of reach, from the one it needs.

Agonising with loss and worry,
This terrestrial heart becomes damaged, a flurry.

Lost in a storm of jealousy and fear,
Thorns not petals drawing hidden tears.

The twist and torsion of mind and soul
Absorbing every thought, consciousness, whole.

Becomes a puppet for joy and pleasure,
Adoration and denial in equal measure.

Transformed into a different form,
Stripped of assets, now reborn

To suit the mould of the ideal,
No longer understanding what is real.

Until the tormented soul it breaks,
A dawn of realisation, it awakes.
Seeing clearly all sides of the arrow
That Cupid once drew so straight and narrow.

The damaged heart begins to mend,
To patch its wounds and defend.

Acceptance of what has gone before,
And that, for sanity, is needed no more

The injured soul breaks free from Venus' clutch,
Feeling blood life return with every touch.

Use your wings, fly be free,
Find the heart who lets you be.

Inspired by 'Venus and Cupid' painted by Pontormo

If You Could See Into My Soul

If you could see into my soul
What would you see?
A myriad of fragments,
The person that is me.

The little girl desperate to dance
With music in her soul,
Twirling, flying without a care
Feeling truly whole.

Or would you see the one
who couldn't be set free?
Free to be original,
The one she was meant to be.

The girl who lived by the dictated rules
in every possible way,
Only to find it brought pain and sadness
Almost every single day

The one who knew in her gut
What her life should bring,
Suffocated by those who 'knew'
The best of everything.

The one who finally found her feet
And shouted to the world
"I am She", "This is Me",
To all those lips that curled.

The sideways glances, whispers caught,
Laughing behind her back;
All the while she smiled to herself

Knowing it was them who truly lacked.

The one who found her tribe, her people,
The ones who let her be;
Who saw her, heard her, lifted her up,
And loved her unconditionally.

And comfortable in her skin she smiles,
As the world moves by,
Grabbing every opportunity offered
To live a life that answers "why?"

If you could see into my soul
This is what you would see;
This and much, much more, no doubt,
That makes this human form me.

IT'S IN THE STARS

Only the stars hold the truth
Of what's been and what's to come,
Our human forms transitory
Never intended to be only one.

From where we came we will return
And fill the skies above,
Glorious, brightly shining,
Illustrious astral dust.

FRIEND

The stars drew us together
All those years ago,
A time least expected
No resistance to pause the flow.

A discovery of familiar,
A discovery of the same;
All the stars had to do
Was create the initial flame.

It was never planned for us to be
Together, one, or whole;
More so parts of each other,
Forever connected, a north star hold.

Energy burns bright between us
A firework for the soul,
Sparks light up the mental skies,
A joy to behold.

And as our life on earth continues
on until its end,
I ask the stars for a few more moments
for both of us my friend.

Come Together Again

Two souls living apart for so long
Find each other again; where they belong.
Reignited with love and joy,
Once forgotten, lost in a void.

Energy burns as they twist and turn,
Creating sparks with heat and yearn.
Joined as resplendent horses of the sea,
Tangled, entwined, the perfect fantasy.

Pure, indisputable, exquisite pleasure,
Through invisible bonds, forever tethered.
Silently dancing, freedom and flow,
Twinkling delight, intensifying glow.

The time comes for these souls to part,
Back to the everyday lives that impart.
Feeling the space, a loss, a hole,
Until next time, my beautiful soul.

I See You

I see you.
When I close my eyes,
I see you.
On the boundary of my vision,
I see you.
When I least expect it,
I see you.

But it's not really you that I see.
Oceans swell, leaking memories,
A reminder, bringing a smile to my face.
Numbing the paper cuts on my heart
that slowly repair, leaving faint scars.

But I still see you,
And I will always see you.

Here and now;
Out there, when;
Always.

WALK WITH ME

We walk together but we're always apart.
You, always a few steps in front,
Checking I'm behind you, that I haven't stopped.

Once in a while you'll pause and fall behind,
Distracted by something I don't see.
Something you can't say but that captures you.

Then you run to catch up
And resume your position at the front.
The front runner, the protector,
The one to keep me safe.

Little do you know it's me that keeps you safe,
That's how it is and will always be.
So come, step outside, and walk with me.

THE SOUL

The soul grows with love, nurture and connection.
A new experience, perfect tune, a dance, a suggestion;
Love, harmony, realising destiny,
Lives lived before coming together in harmony.

It was always meant to be this way,
Relentless time spent finding our path, our stay.
And once found again it is stronger than ever before;
Seamless, exciting, fulfilling and more.

And with that 'more', the soul it soars,
High above, twirling, gliding, bird-like shores;
Singing, its joy radiating, impossible to disguise.
Filling the heart, waking the mind, and opening the eyes.

Sun Daisy

At dawn, waiting for the sun
You stand, drawn in,
Enclosed as one.

The sun comes up,
You stretch and yawn,
Making ready your sun ray cup.

As the hours come and pass,
You open up wide
Revealing your face, bold as brass.

Popping candy-coloured pink,
Like blushing girls,
Show dancers all in sync.

All day long you bend and turn
Your face to the sun.
Warmth you fully savour and yearn.

The sun begins to dip and go,
You feel the shade
Bowing back down low.

Your face drops at the nearing loss
Of love and warmth
Wishing Sun's return, whatever the cost.

Night begins slowly to arrive.
You fold and close
And into twilight you dive.

Hidden again while Moon has her time

You sleep waiting to be awakened
Called by Sun's near morning chime.

MANY ROOMS

My mind is a place of many rooms,
Open spaces and deep dark tombs.

Light and airy for the day-to-day,
Windowless caves for those kept at bay.

Memories boxed, pushed away, forgotten,
Heartaches, losses and times begotten.

Never to see the light of day,
From inquisitive watching eyes kept well away.

Hours spent, the mind running and wandering
Through fields of thought, ideas and conjuring.

Happiness, joy, fun and pleasure
The everyday mind chats at its leisure.

And only when no one else is here
Does it dare to tread on ground not near.

Not surface enough for all to see
Those thoughts are treasures unknown to "we".

They are truths, beliefs and honesty,
Of those things about which we dare not breathe.

So the mind creates landscapes for us to see
Meanwhile, no one knows what all may truly be.

Nothing the protective barrier will reveal,
Enshrouded in silence, an impassable seal.

You're welcome to visit many of my rooms,
Look inside me, share, see how I bloom.

But never shall you truly see my depths,
For those tombs and caves are fully kept.

Hidden only for my mind's eye to brave
To touch, remember and take to the grave.

Is This It?

Is this it? Our one single life?
Someone mentioned there could be two,
Maybe even three or four.
Does anybody really know for sure?

If this is it then I need to live it to the max,
No wasting a day, an hour or a minute.
If this is it, I need to make it clear,
I want the best I can possibly get without fear.

Maybe time is short and not to be wasted
Listening to those "who know best",
The "you shoulds", "you coulds",
"What are you doing that for?",
Who would just as quickly shut their door.

If this is it, I've still so much to do,
I can't sit around opinionating with you;
Creating mountains and valleys so deep
That into my shell I have to creep.

I want to explore, feel joy and love,
I want to fly freely, without judgement or jest.
I want to stand against the tide
So I know I've created my own life inside.

Do you really think that this is it?
That we only get one life?
Ah, so we could have others, but not the same,
Our soul reappears but in a different frame.

So that means the body I am currently in
Gets one chance at this thing called 'life',

Because who knows what a next life will bring?
Or if my soul will remember a single thing?

So for now, for today, I need to make memories,
Experience, learn, be present at every moment.
Because once the time comes for my soul to depart
The last thing I want is an empty, grieving heart.

Or a life less lived than it could have been.

And so I look for the good in all.
I look for the things that bring me joy,
That fill my heart with love and peace,
Only that which makes me smile and never cease.

It doesn't always go to plan, but I try,
Because if I give up what would I have?
A life without memories, laughter and love?
And if this is it, then, for me, there is nothing above.

GRANDPA'S STUDY

It always had a musky smell of old books, paper and dust, even though not a speck would be found, apart from dancing in the sunlight strip radiating from the round, porthole window.

Usually fully shut off from the world, today the blind slightly raised brought with it a golden glow, enhancing the treasures held within.

A small step down as I slowly pulled the roller door across as silently as possible so as not to disturb the peace above and below. Because this room was 'off limits', a sanctity, a haven, only meant for one person.

But I slept in the adjoining room and the hidden secrets, books and records were just too tempting for this inquisitive little girl. If I was quiet, quiet as a little mouse, full of stealth, I could visit this forbidden cave of creativity, mystery and indulgence.

On the left of the door were rows and rows of little filing boxes in columns of 10, each labelled in familiar pencilled script. Of course, in alphabetical order and full of 'bits and bobs' crucial to everyday life. Buttons, envelopes, paper clips, tiny pencils, stamp mounts, stamps, stamps, and more stamps! Some waiting to be invited into a cherished album, some that would never gain that privileged status. Staples, typewriter ribbon, each drawer a delight of discovery, fascination and intrigue time and time again.

And then, in front of the back shelves, packed with historical papers, books and maps, there was the real prize, the true reason for crossing the forbidden boundary. The reason for the breaths held, the carefully placed squeaky floorboard avoidance manoeuvres and ears on full alert.

There on the desk, in all its glory, honoured by the deep red 'spinny' chair was... the typewriter.

Something so coveted by its owner, I was only allowed to see it while escorted and never allowed to touch it unless under specific command.

Some of the letters on the keys were so worn you could only tell what they were when you pressed them and saw the evidence from type bar to paper.

The paper roller that clicked as it turned to load and move the intended parchment, the rest positioned to keep it in its rightful place. The ribbon, part used, the only visible evidence of what had been written before.

The joy of even just taking in that magnificent piece made this all worth the nerves. And then there the seat. Oh! The seat! Well worn, on wheels and a spinning base to make any corner, drawer or shelf accessible without having to leave its comfort. Three spins to the left, then three spins to the right to 'unwind'. And then it was time to type, but so gently that not a sound could be heard in case it alerted anyone to the forbidden acts being carried out.

Holding my breath, my finger hovered over the keys. What to write. Maybe a letter of love for this man; stern, staunch and feverishly protective. A man of music, of history, of life experiences never to be asked about or uttered out loud. A man of love rarely demonstrated but always there to those who knew.

As always, no letter came from the heart, just my name, the typewriter keys in order and maybe a test to see what the shift key might deliver.

Holding my breath at the end of each line to pull on the return handle, covering the end to muffle the unmistakable 'ding'.

Did I hear movement? Voices?

I crept over to the porthole window to have a look. The visitors were leaving. My time was up.

I had a few moments to remove my evidence, shut the opened drawers, and sneak back through the roller door.

Breath held, I turned the paper roller to remove my script, something to secrete under my pillow and look at that night by the light of my window and the roadside lights; delighting in my secret little journey into that mysterious and intriguing world.

Was that the front door shutting? I could hear my grandma walking back to the dining room to clear the cups, saucers and cake plate. My grandpa speaking, but not helping. He's "off to do some research…"

That's my cue; he was on his way up to his study. If I was caught there, I would be in serious bother. I tried to move a bit more quickly. Could I jump the squeaky floor? Yes! Landing like a feather on safe ground. Just the door to navigate, I rolled it as slowly as possible to keep its silence. But then it jammed! Listing to one side as it stalled.

I start to panic, my breath rushing. Any minute I'd hear him on the sixth stair, the one no one can ever avoid, and which acted like a siren warning if you're out of bed or going somewhere you shouldn't be.

I worked with the door again. This time it glided open, not too far, but far enough for me to squeeze through. And then I gently returned it.

My heart pounded as the sixth star creaked. I jumped onto my bed, quickly folding my precious piece of swag, sliding it under my pillow. Sitting cross-legged, I reached for my storybook from my windowsill, opening it quickly as Grandpa turned at the top of the stairs.

Opening my bedroom door, he saw me and smiled. "Are you going to help your grandma out in the garden? I think there are some beans to pick for tea."

I smiled at him. How could I not? "Of course," I say, jumping up and giving him a hug on the way through the doorway. A hug that offered him love, a hug that I knew he cherished, a hug that said a quiet "sorry" for crossing his secret threshold and trespassing into his other world, even just for a few moments. A hug that would make him smile, as he always did, when he realised I had visited his study. How? Because he could always see my footprints on the typewriter ribbon.

RAPHAEL WILKINS

Night Walk

"We'll go tonight," said Doug. "The weather's been dry for long enough." That gave me a frisson of anticipation and fear. He started briefing me in a serious and systematic way, beginning with a large-scale map. Then he talked through illustrations in a book showing some techniques and went on to emphasise various points about safety and respect for terrain. After our meal, I changed into the unfamiliar boiler suit, laced up my well-polished boots, gingerly put on my odd-feeling helmet, and picked up the old metal ammo box in which there were some other bits of kit. It felt strange walking through the village dressed like that. Soon we were out of the residential area into an unlit country lane. "No torches," Doug said. "Let your night vision kick in." Gradually, my eyes adjusted to the dark. Cloud covered about half the sky; stars in the clear half lit the middle-distance landscape surprisingly well. Shadows near-to were a different matter: pools of inky blackness which made me feel dizzy and disorientated.

Doug turned left onto a footpath which rose up a slope: an uneven earth track beside a dry-stone wall at the edge of a field. Towards the crest of the hill, the silhouette of farm buildings appeared off to the left.

"Try not to set the dogs barking," Doug advised. I didn't know how to do that except by willing them not to, staying silent and walking steadily. One half-hearted "woof" and we were past. The path started descending into a valley. There were more trees here, and the ground more uneven, especially as the gradient became steeper.

We were working our way down the valley side, finding good footing and holding onto convenient boulders and tree branches, when a searchlight penetrated the night sky. The effect was scary: I knew it couldn't really be anything to do with us, but I felt hunted and wanted to hide as the beam silently swept over us and onwards. What could it be? We rested for a moment, watching. The beam

174

resolved itself into two beams, moving down the opposite hillside: a vehicle's headlamps - I had never before realised how powerful they were.

"Light pollution," said Doug disapprovingly as we waited for our night vision to return.

The path became easier and levelled out. I could hear running water. The path joined a lane by a stone bridge, which we crossed. This was where the vehicle had passed. The river was quite substantial at this point, and its bed stony and uneven. Doug indicated a path to the left on the opposite bank, which soon came among mature trees. It was now hard to see much, but the path was broad enough to walk abreast and smooth underfoot. We crossed a small tributary ditch, then Doug led the way up the valley side to the right. I needed the heavy tread of my boots to cope with the gradient, but there was more starlight here. The ground dipped downwards for some yards. In front of us was a cliff with a gaping dark mine entrance.

We sat and fiddled with our acetylene lamps, moving the lever to let water drip onto the carbide crystals, then when the smell of gas came through, using the built-in flint to strike a long, slender white flame. Doug reminded me to watch my footing on the rocky floor of the adit, then led me down. At first, the passage sloped downwards at about half the gradient of a domestic staircase, then levelled off after 100 yards or so. The passage was about eight feet high in the centre and five or six feet wide, but it was rough-hewn irregularly out of limestone, so these dimensions varied. The air was cool and damp. Our acetylene lamps provided adequate light, especially when they were both pointing in the same direction. After walking carefully over the uneven and rock-strewn floor of the passage for several hundred yards, we came to a junction configured roughly like an elongated capital 'X', at which we made our arrival from the 'seven o'clock' position. Doug stopped here to do some explaining, his voice echoing dramatically.

"In wet weather, there can be several inches of water here and more down there," indicating the five o'clock tunnel. "The furthest extent and greatest variety of features are that way," indicating two o'clock. He described tall chambers and a small turquoise pond. "But we are doing the short tour today," and led the way slightly uphill towards the eleven o'clock tunnel.

This soon shrank to a hands-and-knees crawl, heads down, shoulders and hips rubbing the walls. In the confined space, the lamps seemed brighter. The tunnel walls and roof were lumpy and nearly white. The floor was quite smooth, with a thin covering of muddy material in places. The dramatic effect of this crawl was heightened by how the tunnel twisted and turned. In this winding passage, I thought of boyhood treasure-hunting stories and lost all sense of direction. Since entering the mine, I had been looking out for any signs of lead, but every speck of it had been worked out long ago.

I was also thinking about how this trip might lead to others. I had heard Doug talk about natural caves, rock climbing, watching the sun rise from a high peak, navigating unfamiliar country without a map, sleeping under the stars in a space emergency blanket... My mind drifted on to the possibilities for exciting and challenging experiences if I played my cards right. If this was just for starters, the taster, then what followed could be quite something.

The tunnel opened out and we stood up. We were in a tall fissure, about five feet wide at the base and narrowing upwards into a muddle of shadows. The ground was of very uneven sloping mud. The fissure seemed to stretch some way ahead, but a few yards in front of us was a round black hole covering most of the width of the floor.

"Remember about chimneying," Doug said. 'I'll go first and guide you down. The next level is not far below. The chimney narrows as you go." He settled himself into the hole, shoulders braced against one wall, feet against the other, and started edging downwards while I watched anxiously. When he stood up at the bottom, his head was only four or five feet below, so I became more confident that I could manage this, and once settled in the hole and braced in position, I felt surprisingly secure. I inched down until the gap started narrowing.

"OK, you'll need to change from feet to knees, but give me your left foot first."

I felt him grab my left boot and guide it to a good, firm hold; shortly after, he did the same with my right. It was a relief a few slithers later to get both feet on the ground.

We were standing in a passage proceeding in both directions, roughly underneath the one we had left.

"OK, lead the way in that direction," said Doug. I felt pretty good about the manoeuvre we had just completed and about being in front. The passage was just big enough to walk in a crouched posture. After proceeding in that way for a while, daydreaming pleasantly, it was a bit of a shock to find my lamp shining on a stout metal gate, padlocked with a heavy chain. I exclaimed, checked it was really locked, and wondered, if we had to turn back, how we would get up to the level from which we had descended.

"It was gated some months ago," Doug said. "Probably because this adit can be seen from the path."

After letting me stew a moment, he said,

"Time to learn another skill." The gate was rectangular, but the passage was irregular: there was a gap of several inches at the bottom of its unhinged side. It also moved about four inches each way on its chain. Doug removed several stones, which were already loose, from the ground at that corner and swept aside some smaller stones, adding several more inches to the gap. "Slip your helmet off a minute, now lay down on your left side, stretch your left arm ahead, right arm back, slope your shoulders, tilt your head to your left arm, and wriggle through." Following these instructions, while Doug held the gate in a certain position, I was surprised to be able to make tight progress through what had seemed an impossibly narrow gap.

Doug followed and we replaced the stones. I continued to lead for another fifty yards or so when the air changed. It was not a case of seeing the light at the end of the tunnel but smelling the smell: a pungent blend of rotting leaves and wood, fungi and warm soil as we emerged and stood upright in the starlit night. I remarked on this.

"Yes," said Doug. "The world we live in smells rotten; you only notice it after breathing clean cave air."

As we walked back, I couldn't shake Doug's comment about "the world we live in" out of my mind. I kept wondering if he was implying a more general point about his attitude towards the everyday world: its limitations and boredom. He seemed to follow a different dimension in which he could come alive: I wanted that too.

GUN RUNNER

Dear Roger   16 March 1974
Would you be free to meet me at 1.00 pm next Tuesday in the foyer
bar at the Intercontinental Hotel? I have developed a funding source
which we can use to help our friends up north.
Yours ever,
Ben

Dear Darling
Arrived safely in Nairobi. Spatters of rain when I came out of the
airport this morning: I didn't think of rain when I was choosing my
clothes for the trip. Taxi drove past brown savanna, acacia trees, dark
green bushes, red earth and scrubby verges. In the city, went past the
parliament buildings: the hotel is just around the corner.

Although the hotel is a modern tower block, it is designed to give
a nice colonial feel, especially on the ground floor, where the foyer
has a curved line of massive buff pillars. A wood-panelled corridor
leads to the restaurant where I have enjoyed Nile Perch and beef stew
and good Kenyan tea. My room has a floor-to-ceiling window
looking out over the city centre, which is neat and spacious, ceramic
tiled floor with rugs, and a lot of African-style fabrics on the chairs
and cushions. The altitude makes me want to sleep a lot. This
afternoon, I reacquainted myself with the company's Kenya office: a
miniature version of the London office in a bit of a time warp, but
everyone is nice and friendly. The office is outside the city centre:
the block it is in is modern and in good order, but it is in a mixed area
with a lot of hummocky waste ground. The road to it is just a beaten-
earth track. The direction signs at junctions are like the ones we used
to see in country lanes: whiteboards with finger-shaped ends pointing
in each direction. I have also bumped into an old school friend who
lives here trading in this and that.
Love, Ben

Dear Roger

Thanks for our discussion. I'm glad you are up for it. To confirm, you will procure the equipment from local sources in nearly-new condition. First payment when our friends have seen a sample and are happy to proceed; main payment on delivery of main batch of goods.

Yours ever,

Ben

Dear Shadrach

I can get what you want, for a small consideration of course, and if you could do me a little favour in return. Could we discuss if I come to Juba at the weekend? Perhaps your assistant could pick me up from Logali House if you tell me the best day and time.

Comradely regards,

Ben

Dear Darling

I think my assignment here will last about a month. When I am clearer about the end date, perhaps we could fix up a short relaxing break in Cayman if that would suit? I had a nice weekend: got to fly in a small plane up to Juba. The plane flew low enough for me to get good views of everything. The terrain north of Nairobi is very varied: circles of cultivated land surrounded by dark green forest, bright green fields on the lower ground and in the insides of river meanders. The settlements are dispersed and very low density, usually scattered along a straight earth road. A lot of the huts are roofed with blue plastic. I had good views of the rift valley and a massive lake. The uplands are weird: dark green and deeply dissected, a bit like looking into a rock pool. Then there was savannah, tinged ochre and purple, so I knew I was in Sudan. Saw the Nile snaking in the distance; the pilot made a very steep descent to the airstrip. A heavy shower was just ending, so I had to splash through red muddy puddles to the terminal hut, which was packed with people sheltering and a lot of soldiers in combat dress.

Juba doesn't seem to have normal urban form: it seems to be a patchwork of different kinds of land use all muddled up. There are some old roads with tarmac and proper signs that look as if they date from the colonial period, but most of the roads are earth with very deep ruts and potholes. Everywhere, there are patches of traditional huts, round with mud walls and thatched rooves, many leaning or falling to pieces. I had hoped to enjoy standing on the banks of the Nile in my David Livingstone outfit but didn't manage to get round to it. Perhaps another time.

Love,

Ben

Dear Roger

To set up your first payment, I have opened an ordinary personal deposit account for you at the local bank here, for which no proof of identification is required. The account is in the name of Mr A. I. Blades. The company's computer will credit the agreed sum, if it were sentient, it would believe it is settling an invoice from the firm A1 Blades for the provision of band-saw equipment.

Yours ever,

Ben

Dear Roger

No, not at all: no fake invoices, no hassle, no paper trail of any kind.

Yours,

Ben

Dear Roger

Curiosity killed the cat! The company makes computerised batch payments every Thursday. A computer payment coding slip is completed for each invoice. These are batched. The person making up the batch uses the adding machine to check that the total of the coding slips matches the total of the invoices. The two adding machine rolls, the coding slips and invoices are then checked by a colleague. I will make up a batch of invoices of similar size to your payment, complete your coding slip, and simply add the amount to the adding machine check of the invoice totals. I will pass them to a colleague who I know won't check thoroughly once she has seen that the two totals tally. Then when the copies of the remittance advice come back, I will destroy the one for that payment. So no paper record. The worst that could happen is that a future auditor might be puzzled but would not have any pointer as to where to start looking. Relax!

Yours ever,

Ben

Dear Roger

Great to know you are ready to pass over the sample for inspection. Can we go on an excursion this weekend? If you are happy to drive us up alongside Lake Turkana with the sample goods in a nice, neat crate, we can meet our friends at an exact distance beyond Kakuma. They will use the coloured rags on trees method of liaison.

Yours ever,

Ben

Dear Shadrach

So glad you like the sample item of equipment. I need to receive your goodwill gift before we go any further if you don't mind: a small fraction of the worth of the goods, I'm sure you will agree.

Comradely regards,

Ben

Dear Roger

Our friends liked your equipment. Congratulations, Mr Blades! Your first payment from the company is ready to collect. Please now prepare to deliver the main consignment. I have opened a new account in the name of Mr A. C. E. Steel. This time, Ace Steel is supplying the company with some nice girders.

Yours ever, Ben

Dear Roger

It's great to know you are ready. I will alert our friends. I'll see you off, but you go on your own this time. Go on the same route as before to Kakuma, then keep on the same highway to Lockichokia. It turns into a dirt road beyond the settlement, and within a mile, there is a more minor track heading off to the left. Take that and follow it for a couple of miles; at the crossroads, turn left again on a rough seasonal track heading towards the hills, to a point about five miles short of the border with Uganda. Take a track on the right, which leads across an open section of the Sudanese border, take the left fork, which connects with the more obvious dirt track leading to Loming, where our friends are in control. They will meet you just outside the settlement; please give them my kindest regards, and I wish you a pleasant scenic journey.

Yours ever,

Ben

Dear Darling

I have booked leave for the period 11th to 15th. Do you mind making your own way to Cayman? I don't want a lot of boring questions at Heathrow, so will come via Muscat and Frankfurt in time to meet you at the airport. We can stay in our usual place and benefit from the wonderful cocktails. It will be nice to see the turtles on the beach

again, to laze on the white sand, and I will need to do some banking.
Love,
Ben

Dear Sir
You will have noted that I have emptied my deposit account, and this may now be closed.
Yours faithfully,
A. C. E. Steel

Dear Shadrach
So pleased you have what you wanted. I am sure the Land Rover and trailer will also be useful for your important work. Thank you for dealing with the courier in the manner agreed, thereby demonstrating the effectiveness of the equipment.
Comradely regards,
Ben

STANLEY AND SALMA

Her picture caught Stanley's attention when he clicked on the connection request. Smiling, saucy eyes peeped up at the camera at an angle that emphasised her cheekbones under a swirl of dark, wavy hair. Stanley hesitated: he only accepted connection requests if they were relevant. The profile said she ran a school in the far north of India. Stanley was getting ready to do a two-week project in India: an unexpected post-retirement consultancy with an organisation he hadn't worked with before. He was not going to Salma's town, although that had been suggested originally. So this link could be relevant. Was it despite, or because of, her pretty face that he clicked 'accept'? Immediately after 'You and Salma are now connected', she sent a friendly message saying that she was part of his forthcoming project and would be working with him in Gurgaon and Hyderabad. Stanley sweated: how was he to know? What if he had dismissed the connection request? Then glowed: a project was always more enjoyable with a nice colleague.

Stanley landed in Delhi and found the terminal familiar from previous visits. The drive to Gurgaon took an hour: he had last been there three years previously but did not recognise anything. New buildings and unfinished tower blocks were everywhere. The no-man's land between highway and building line was filled with shanties, crude shops, vending carts, rickshaws and cows. He was lodged at the Taj Vivanta Hotel: new, luxurious, and by its own description, 'Uber-indulgent, an Indo-Islamic architectural marvel'. Which is true, he thought, looking from his high-grade room at the Delhi elevated metro and signs of booming economic development.

Rajiv, the boss of the organisation running the project, had arranged a lunch for him at his apartment to meet some people. The roads were congested and potholed: they had been designed for village and small-town use. Rajiv's apartment was in a gated complex. It was extensive, stylish and with a panoramic view. It was

185

bustling with people: a mixture of family and employees, animatedly talking in groups. Rajiv introduced some, and some introduced themselves, including a young woman, but in the hubbub, Stanley didn't catch her name.

A minute later, Rajiv led him back to the same young woman, saying, "Have you met Salma? She will be working with you."

Stanley apologised, blaming his poor hearing. She's nothing like her studio portrait, he thought, but fine-featured: different from different angles.

"And that's my husband over there", Salma said, pointing to a young man.

The first assignment was at a school in Gurgaon. The training room was a cool basement underneath a lily pond. Everything about the project was new, so the team had to concentrate. Salma sat to one side, busy with administration. After a few days, Rajiv took Stanley to Mumbai, which he had not visited before. It was different from anything he had seen in other parts of India. Parts reminded him of Lagos: areas of obvious poverty, the long coastline and bridge sweeping across the inlet. The central business district looked like Manhattan. Parts of the coastal frontage reminded him of Brighton: a sophisticated and bustling seaside resort. The locality of the hotel was like Mayfair. The work in Mumbai went smoothly, and on a free afternoon, Rajiv took Stanley on a walking tour of the old town. Sweating in his shirtsleeves, Stanley saw the attraction of the place to tourists. Rajiv was staying longer; Stanley left early in the morning to fly to Hyderabad. On the taxi ride, he noticed that the traffic lights shut down overnight to prevent unnecessary waiting - a good system.

At Hyderabad, Stanley was relieved to meet up with Salma, whose flight from Delhi landed shortly after his. She emerged like a film star in big sunglasses and waved to identify herself. In the car, it became clear that the office had muddled up the Westin Hotel, the intended lodging, which was high grade, in a high-tech city and very near the training venue, with the Best Western – lower grade and

186

about 50 minutes drive from the venue. It turned out to have numerous inadequacies. Hyderabad comprised a network of separate towns: the venue was a beautifully designed modern school, approached by complicated cart-tracks in a traditional small town.

Salma was always busy: among other things, she had only recently joined the organisation and was finding her way in a new line of work and anxious to do well. Her smartphone rarely rested for more than a few minutes. The unplanned daily commute provided their only social time. Salma was relaxed and friendly, and happy to chat about herself.

In the small spaces between her phone usage, Stanley learnt that she was 35, a Muslim, and a member of the former royal family of one of the princely states. She had been married at an early age to a millionaire and had two teenage daughters. After that marriage ended, she had married a childhood playmate. Stanley formed an impression that he was awkward and needed mothering. Stanley also learnt why Salma needed to do so much telephoning. It was all in Hindi, so he was dependent on her explanations. On a range of small domestic matters, she liked to consult with her sisters, her mother, her mother-in-law, and her ex-husband's mother. On one occasion, Salma told Stanley that her mother was cooking soup for her husband, and she had needed to give her very detailed instructions about how he liked it. Stanley knew when Salma was speaking with her husband because her voice took on cooing, purring, wheedling tones of besotted adoration. Sometimes he teased her about this acting.

But for most of the time on these drives, Stanley was left to amuse himself by looking out of the window at expanses of scrub and trees, with dramatic rock formations like tors or perched boulders, while Salma's finger-tip smeared the greasy surface of her smartphone. The Hyderabad assignment finished, group photographs were taken, and Stanley and Salma tidied up, ready to go straight to the airport.

When they went outside with their cases, the taxi had not arrived.

Salma sat on a low wall and immersed herself in her smartphone. Stanley stood with her, his emotions divided. He disliked being kept waiting in the hot sun with a companion who right now was not being very companionable: he assumed Salma was berating the taxi driver in Hindi. And yet here he was, being paid to spend time in this exotic garden with this amazing girl, this woman, this princess with her big diamond, whose stylish clothes showed off her toned shoulders and arms while breeze fingered her long glossy hair. When at last he had her attention, Stanley asked about a nearby tree which had leaves like Acacia, beans like Catalpa, and brilliant red flowers. Salma said it was a Gulmohar, and Stanley made her write it in his notebook, which she did in neat capital letters: his only sample of her writing.

The taxi came; for much of the drive, Salma haggled with the driver over the extent to which he had been overcharging her.

At the airport, the check-in clerk said, "I am upgrading the lady to premium economy so that she can sit with you."

At the last possible moment before take-off, Salma switched off her phone. Seeing this, Stanley put away his book. Salma talked, and with Stanley's active encouragement, she talked for the whole flight about life and likes and relationships. On landing, she led the way to where her husband would pick them up. Her husband had been annoyed by her trip and had refused to take her to the airport, and she had been determined to take a taxi home, but during their various conversations in the meantime, he had insisted on this pick-up, and she had agreed.

Stanley had expected Delhi to be cooler than the south, but the night air was hot and humid.

Salma became edgy; then, "That's him!" and their reunion happened while Stanley put his case in the boot and sat in the back seat. Salma burbled a lot of nervous nonsense to her husband about the hotel in Hyderabad, saying this was what they had discussed during the flight. Soon they came to the Lemon Tree Hotel, where Stanley was lodging because of its convenience for his morning flight to London. Would she be coming in to check the booking? No, of course not. This was goodbye.

"Goodbye," Salma said, reaching her hand back between the seats. When Stanley took it in his, she gripped it tightly, in a pulsating way, for several seconds.

Next morning, Stanley was given a free upgrade to business class for his flight to London. He wanted to tell Salma about this happy end to the trip. At home, he sent Rajiv his report, copying Salma in, and a brief note to her thanking her for her support. Would she reply with a similar business pleasantry? With a tremor of excitement, he saw a reply almost immediately. She had written, 'Thank you for being such a sweetheart'.

Freudian Slip

C lement Freud twisted his body around towards the press, away from the chairman, and contorted his rubbery features into a dramatic comic version of an infant biting on a sour lemon. Thus, he expressed what he thought of the chairman and the proceedings of the committee, of which he was a member.

This was in the spring of 1985 before Commons business was televised. It was also before digital document production. Stenographers sat and clacked away, producing the verbatim record, which we tidied up using proof correction marks. To get the amount of paperwork required into meetings, sometimes I used a traditional porter's trolley, humping it down the steps at the old Westminster tube station.

Joining the House of Commons staff in my early thirties, on a short contract, and then daring to pace its gilded corridors made me feel like a goggle-eyed rustic. Being there, but not really there: in a sort of dream, because only members can truly be there. I could stand behind the speaker's chair to listen to interesting debates. Frequently, I was closely proximate to famous people on staircases, in lifts, in the library: such people get used to looking straight through junior staff with whom they are not involved.

Clement Freud, famous for television dog-food adverts, his illustrious ancestor, and his unexpected election as a Liberal MP, was the only name I knew beforehand among the committee members. Somehow, I expected he would be popular: it was a surprise to learn from my boss and from small comments by other committee members that he was disliked for his negativity and lack of commitment.

Committee attendances were recorded by presence in sessions (usually two hours or more), regardless of whether this was for all or part of the session. Clement would routinely come in late, catch the chairman's eye and be allowed to ask the witnesses his question, then leave five minutes later, thus creating a paper trail in Hansard and proceedings that he could pass off as a diligent contribution.

The chairman who courteously bore this misuse was Sir William van Straubenzee. Pickwickian, with his pinstripes and sideburns, elaborate signature and his formal statesmanlike manner, he was too easily written off by some as pompous. Short but commanding while always extremely polite: a lawyer, a churchman, and a former minister of state, he had earned a fair measure of regard. I was happy to imitate some of his careful diplomatic methods in later career phases.

"It makes more impact to understate rather than overstate your case", he would advise. Once, during a conversation about a completely external matter, he said to me, "If you support an organisation, don't act in a way that will tear it down the middle." In committee, which was cross-party but with a built-in government majority, he applied the same rule. "If we push this to a division, we know which way it will go, so let's find a way forward we can all agree." Which he did: every report under his chairmanship was unanimous.

When I started working with the committee, it was involved in a long inquiry into primary education, in between short inquiries and scrutiny sessions with the secretary of state. The justification had been that primary education had not had a thorough examination since the Plowden Report of the sixties, although some suspected that it was a conveniently uncontroversial topic to choose.

That summer - June it would have been, before the recess - the Committee took evidence from primary schools in Oxford; I went with them. For security reasons, they had to be VIP-ed on the train: a strip of red carpet, a guard accompanying. At Oxford, everyone else picked up their cases, but Clement pointedly walked off, leaving his, expecting a member of staff to carry it. I told him to go back and get it. The hotel was perfectly adequate, and the whole group chose the cheap set dinner, but Clement complained about the small size of his room. He had a 'Do you realise I am a hotel critic?' session with the manager and got moved to a suite. He remained prickly throughout the work. "Clement has a bear's head this morning!" the chairman commented. The chairman liked to be very courteous and considerate to anyone we were visiting, and we were a bit on edge in case Clement rocked the boat.

The Summer Recess came and went, and the inquiry ground along. On the 15th of December 1985, on the BBC's *In Committee,* Clement broadcast critical remarks about the chairman's style, the length of the primary education inquiry, and that "We have a fair amount of freebies". He elaborated these views in an interview in *Education,* referring to "pointless trips and junkets", citing the Oxford trip and questioning why it was necessary for the committee "to stay at an exclusive Oxford hotel with wining and dining to match".

Clement's public attack set off a bandwagon of hostile reporting, unleashing an undercurrent of grumbling about a perceived lack of incisiveness of the select committees. The frenetic, partisan and combative style of the previous committee, chaired by Chris Price, cast a long shadow. Clement Freud had served on it, and the contrast between the two committees was the key theme of the *In Committee* programme. The chairman had refused the BBC's invitation to join that discussion. Harry Greenway did take part: he was a senior Conservative member of both the current committee and its predecessor. He defended the committee's decision to look in depth at primary education and pointed out that Clement had wanted that inquiry to cover additional elements that would greatly have extended its length. He noted that the committee's time had not been exclusively devoted to that inquiry and considered Mr Freud's attendance had been so minimal he was not well placed to criticise. Mr Greenway accepted that the chairman had been "very laidback", but "I don't think anyone could be fairer in the way he brings people in…he has shown none of the ruthlessness and challenge towards committee members that his predecessor showed all the time."

For the permanent staff, the manner of Freud's speaking out was scandalous. It also threatened their own professional reputations. We had a set of small offices on the sixth floor of St Stephen's House, along the front, giving views through the bomb-blast curtains of the Thames and County Hall beyond. There was also a disgusting old kitchen at the back. My boss strode around this domain agitatedly, saying, "I'm not having my committee becoming a *cause celebre*!". He was torn because he had worked with and liked the previous committee and was himself frustrated by the committee's modest productivity and punch. We did some analysis of the committee's output of short and longer inquiries since the start of the current parliament, which was actually pretty respectable. It just felt lacklustre to those who had known the contrast.

I had no view either way: I was an outsider, there as a specialist, although I was sure every member of the committee knew more than me. I saw depth and weight in the consensus-building: I had read that some of the reports of the previous committee had been written by a small sub-group then forced through on the casting vote of the chair. But the big question hanging in the air along our corridor was how the chairman would decide to handle the situation.

The allegation resented most because it was ridiculous was that of extravagance. It was obvious to the committee members themselves and to parliamentary staff that the committee must have been the most ascetic and skinflint public body ever to travel on official business. But some members were also affronted that Clement had been personally derogatory about the chairman, saying that he liked "pomp and ceremony … he's had his little day … he chairs the Committee as if he was chairing the Synod", and so on.

Sir William's lawyerly tactics were impeccable. There was no outburst of indignation, no participation in media debate, no public comment of any kind. The next meeting of the committee took place as if nothing had happened, with Clement in attendance. I was amazed how MPs absorbed such brass neck. The committee chose not, in its formal capacity, to comment on its expenditure or on Clement's breach of protocol in taking matters to the media without first discussing them internally. Nor would Sir William be drawn into commenting on issues of his personal style: "None of us can afford to be too thin-skinned if we want to work in this place". Instead, he skilfully got the committee to confine its attention to the central matter of the progress of the primary education inquiry. On that, the chairman, no doubt having had some private one-to-one conversations, steered the production of a minute, reaffirming that the inquiry would continue to adhere to the schedule originally agreed for it. This decision was supported by every member of the committee, including Clement Freud.

This brief, low-key minute did little to stifle the broader debate that the incident had generated. While respecting the chairman's diplomatic victory, the other committee members wanted to counter Clement's wider accusations. All the members except for the chairman and Clement Freud signed a letter which was published on the 21st of February 1986 in the *Times Educational Supplement*. In it, they argued the unfairness of Clement's views, pointing out his lack of contribution, pointing out how he had complained because the Oxford hotel had not been of higher grade, and in particular, defending Sir William van Straubenzee's chairmanship. The *Financial Times* picked up on this letter and described it as 'an unprecedented public rebuke' for Mr Freud.

GOODBYE YORKSHIRE ROSE

"Along the Road to Withernsea" the theme of the rhyme[1]
That kindled imagination in my boyhood time
Finding a map to locate the lilting lonely tale
"No wonder, walking there, that the man was sad and pale!"

Now roke stings my grizzled chin and smarts my rheumy eye
The track runs like an arrow under Hockney's poles and sky
Warm within with love, plans and good things to remember
A bambi bounds through flattened grass of dank December.

Wind-bent bushes, gnarled lichened branches brittle and bare
Reflect and ponder by sodden carr with darting hare
Jasper-littered beige sand, chert, coral and slumped red clay
Tussocks tinged with pink and gold at the turn of the day.

Seagulls screek and skim the spume of lilac leaden sea
And walking with me by the waves is the child I used to be:
Bony knees on a rag rug with atlas at my side
Finger pointing to the place where I found my dark-haired bride[2].

---

1. 'Black and White', by H H Abbott, in L D'O Walters (1920) *An
Anthology of Recent Poetry,* London: Harrap.

2. Mary Harvey, born Withernsea, 1947, died Barnard Castle, 2020.

Printed in Poland
by Amazon Fulfillment
Poland Sp. z o.o., Wrocław

27176247R00114